GHOST GIRL

Ennis, County Clare, Ireland

2005

GHOST GIRL

Helena McEwen

BLOOMSBURY

Acknowledgements

Hawthornden Foundation, K. Blundell Trust, Santa Maddalena
Foundation, Victoria Hobbs, Alexandra Pringle, Mary Tomlinson,
Barbara Turner, Richard and Marigold Farmer, Armando Cruz
Sanchez, Maria Ines Correa, Ginny Struthers, Margaret Stourton,
Matthew Kneale, Kirsty Hesketh, Frances Ham, Louise Page,
Annie Gillies, Anjum Moon.

First published in Great Britain 2004
This paperback edition published 2005

Copyright © 2004 by Helena McEwen

The moral right of the author has been asserted

A CIP catalogue record for this book
is available from the British Library

Bloomsbury Publishing Plc, 38 Soho Square, London W1D 3HB

ISBN 0 7475 7410 3
9780747574101

10 9 8 7 6 5 4 3 2 1

All papers used by Bloomsbury Publishing are natural,
recyclable products made from wood grown in well-managed forests.
The manufacturing processes conform to the
environmental regulations of the country of origin.

Printed by Clays Ltd, St Ives plc

www.bloomsbury.com/helenamcewen

To my sisters, Mary Christian, Katie and Isabella.

PART ONE

'OK, tell me three things you like about it, then I'll shut up.'

'There aren't three.'

'There must be. You can count food.'

Black-iron leaves hold up a globe of pale-pink light that turns my shadow turquoise on the pavement.

'Here's the right place,' says Very, climbing some steps on to a bench that looks across the dark river. She gets out her drawing book, a bottle of black ink, and a paintbrush with a bamboo handle.

'Olive,' I say, sitting down beside her.

I watch as Very turns the white of the paper into the lit-up beads strung across the bridge against the black-ink sky, and into bright ripples of reflected light in the black-ink river.

'Olives?' she says, watching her paintbrush.

'No, Olive, I like her.'

I could tell she was new too, and terrified like I was, standing in the supper queue with her hands in a twisted plait, looking about with those magnified eyes.

Very tears off the picture carefully and gives it to me to hold while it dries.

She had numbers in those eyes. They lit her up, measurements, distances, the speed of light, twenty-three times round the earth in one second.

And she loves the sun.

I watch as Very draws the moon with a stick of charcoal. I look up and see it shining across the river.

When the other two arrived, girls shouted, 'Queue-bargers!' from behind.

'The new girls saved our places, didn't you,' they said, and Olive and I both nodded that we had.

Eliza sang under her breath, 'Little new girls do what they're to-old,' and I didn't want to remember that.

'Olive what, anyway,' said Eliza.

'Olive Burnham,' whispered Olive.

'I thought you were going to say Olive Green!' said Eliza.

'I thought you were going to say Olive Oyl,' said Pen. 'You've got the right hairstyle!'

I look at the black water with the sleeping boats sliding to and fro on the wake of a night-time police boat. Very is hurrying to draw it into her picture as it moves across the page shattering the bright ripples of reflected moon.

In fact what Olive likes best are the stars, their size, their names Bellatrix and Betelgeuse in the constellation of Orion, and Bellatrix has a diameter of two hundred and forty million miles, which is only just under three times the distance between us and the sun, she told me, her eyes blinking a lot.

Very blows the charcoal dust off the page. She has a smudge down the side of her nose and black fingers.

She looks at me and her eyes are lit by the pink street lights.

'Second thing?'

4

I shake my head.

'Think about it,' she says.

I scan through the days and nights of my memory, trying to avoid the things I don't want to see.

That first night when I lay in bed listening to the creaking partitions and waiting for the lights to go out, breathing not too deeply so I wouldn't disturb the wrench that happened in my throat when they said, 'Don't come all the way downstairs, we can say goodbye here,' and they'd walked along the yellow strip of carpet down the centre of Yellow D that stood for dormitory, and past the colourless virgin with her arms outstretched. There had been a little tapping on the wood behind the yellow curtain. It took a few taps before I thought to say, 'Yes,' in a whisper.

She'd drawn back the curtain and asked permission to come in when she was already through, and to sit down as she sat down on the bed. They were all dressed the same and it was hard to tell them apart, you had to look at their eyes, and the shape their hidden bodies made the habit; tall habits, short habits, fat habits, stooped habits, all black and down to the ground with a veil that got swept behind like long hair, only a triangle of face showing, and hands emerging from white cuffs.

She sat on my bed looking at me with her eyebrows raised in a question.

'Do you know how to finish the day, dear?' she asked, looking at me with her eyes shut.

I shook my head.

'No, Sister.'

'You should finish the day by kneeling down and saying your night prayers.'

'Yes, Sister, I did say them.'

'Good child, and after your night prayers what should you do?'

Again she looked at me with her eyes shut, but the eyelashes fluttered.

'Get into bed?'

'After your night prayers you should observe due modesty in going to bed . . .' she said, lowering her eyes.

I waited for her to continue.

'. . . occupy yourself with thoughts of death . . .' There was another pause. 'And endeavour to compose yourself to rest at the foot of the cross and give your last thoughts to our crucified saviour.'

She waited a long time with her eyes shut.

When she opened her eyes I got a shock because I was watching them.

'Yes, Sister.'

'All right, goodnight, my child.'

'Goodnight, Sister.'

She seemed to be waiting at the curtain.

'Thank you, Sister.'

She nodded and slipped through.

'Well?' says Very, rubbing out a big patch in the centre of her page, and flicking away the bits of rubber. The bright moon has gone behind an orange cloud and the sky has turned brown. She sighs – her drawing is not working.

'Don't you have a second thing, Cath?'

I look at her head bending over the picture and all that straggly hair going in her eyes, the charcoal smudged down the side of her nose. I'm so relieved to be with her.

'The river.'

'This one?'

'No, at school, the second thing.'

'You're not allowed there, are you?'

'No, but I sneaked there.'

'You can't count out of bounds.'

The out of bounds, the not allowed, the forbidden river is where I feel at home. Like I feel at home with Very. Through the wet ferns that splash your face with water droplets, and under them the blue grass with rows of water beads, the nettles and tall willow herb covered in fluffy seeds, their long thin leaves turning orange and red next to the violet flowers, through the grass and thistles and down to the stones. The large smooth stones and the black mud, and if you take your shoes and socks off and wade in you can see the dark-brown water turns your feet deep-orange.

The water froths when it has been raining and rises up the bank.

'D'you sneak there a lot?'

'Only did it once.'

'Well, the river doesn't count. Think of something else.'

I watch her black hand, the charcoal snaps, Very spits on to the page and starts drawing with her fingers.

She'd come the next morning too. She walked into my dream and I nearly screamed because she was sitting on my bed, looking at me with her eyes shut. But I gasped instead and tried to blink away the monkey with the blue tongue.

'Do you know how to begin your day, my child?'

'No, Sister.'

'You should begin the day by making the sign of the cross as soon as you wake in the morning' – she took my hand and helped me make the sign of the cross – 'saying,' "Oh my God . . ."' She stopped and nodded to let me repeat it. '"I offer my heart and soul to you."'

'Do you know how you should rise in the morning, dear?'

'No, Sister.'

'You should rise in the morning diligently,' she said, bowing her head, 'dress yourself modestly,' another bow, 'and kneel down to say your morning prayers.'

'Yes, Sister, thank you, Sister.'

Very closes her book. She looks at me and chews her cheek.

'Come on. I'll show you the sculpture,' she says, and pats me on the back.

We walk along by the twinkling Thames, Very

pointing out the four upside-down table-legs of Batter-sea Power Station. The leaves are falling in the water although there is no wind. We cross the road. Outside a tall glass building is a boy suspended in midair, his arms and legs outstretched, holding the fin of a dolphin with one hand. Very thinks it is sentimental. I think it's the most beautiful thing I've ever seen.

We walk back through the dark buildings, glowing with rectangles of coloured light, yellow, pink, red, green, depending on the curtains. They make the night look cosy.

I think of the biology lab and the copper taps with verdigris in the cracks, the coiled orange tube, a faint smell of gas, a yellow lick of flame and the quivering blue eye. And I think of Miss Tweedie who isn't a nun, who told us we're made of spinning atoms, but mostly space. You're a miniature universe, she said, and it made me breathe in to think of all that space inside me, and she smiled her red smile. We made acid drops in her class and she even took us to the stone staircase of the Upper School so we could pour dry ice down the steps and see it rise in clouds of white mist.

'Miss Tweedie.'

'What?'

'The chemistry teacher. I like her.'

'Glad to hear it. That's two things.'

She opens the front door and we quietly sneak up the stairs, so as not to wake the old man and his housekeeper, who live underneath. Mrs McGonogall is small with a hunched back and yellow wizened skin, but eyes so bright they twinkle like a child's.

'Come and visit, darlin',' she'd said. 'Come and have a sit in the garden under the pear tree and I'll make us a nice cup of tea.'

'Thank you,' I'd said, and her hand had reached up far longer than you'd expect from such a short body, reached up along the banister slowly, like a spider's leg, and given my back a stroke.

'There, honey, I hardly ever get to talk with the young ones – it's just that old bastard to keep me company.' She'd smiled a yellow smile.

We clamber up the narrow stairs, into the little room with too-big furniture. A black desk under the window, a long square sofa under a huge gilt mirror, a large chest with faded painted flowers, two small chests of drawers with loose gold knobs, some of them missing, so you can't open them any more.

'D'you want tea?'

I'd considered the chest but when I saw the loose gold knob I'd stuffed it all in the drawer and pulled the knob off, the brown pleated skirt, the yellow-and-brown tie, the blazer, the white shirt, the brown socks. They were unreachable now.

'Do you? I've got biscuits.'

'Mmm.'

I'd worn it on the train, of course. Very said she couldn't tell which one I was when she collected me from the station. I had to call out to her. 'Very! Very, it's me!' She was looking at all their faces with a frown, trying to see mine. But then the frown broke, I could see her eyes all lit up. Her face was smiling.

'There you are!'

We'd come out on to the thundering road.

She'd said, 'Let's go there,' pointing over the road.

The cars were zooming. 'Wimpy Bar' was written in huge red letters. I'd screwed my face up.

'Oh just a quick bite, I'm starving.'

'All right,' I said, 'but I'm not eating anything.'

So we crossed the road from the station.

'Light the heater if you like. The matches are in the jar,' Very calls down the stairs.

I can hear the kettle beginning to boil. She bangs down the stairs and into the bedroom.

I didn't like it, still wearing my school uniform. Very was wearing her wellingtons and the turquoise skirt with paint spattered over it, and that striped jersey with holes in the elbows. I suppose her hair wasn't exactly brushed. She was carrying her sketch book and her fingers were covered in charcoal.

'What, scared it'll still be alive?' She'd winked at me as she pushed the dark-red door.

Inside it was dingy, the pale-yellow paint was peeling off the walls and the floor looked dirty. Three large photographed hamburgers were lit up behind the counter. The man serving had a gap between his teeth. Very had stood at the counter looking at the photographs and chewing her lip.

'Well, hmm,' she said.

I noticed the man behind the counter look her up and down.

'Shall I have a cheeseburger with fries or double burger?'

The man was coming round the counter shaking his head.

'Which d'you think, Cath . . .'

He was striding towards her.

'. . . you could have a Coke.'

But his hands were on her shoulders and he was shaking his head.

She'd looked surprised, as if he was greeting her, but he was shaking his head.

'No!' he'd said.

'Sorry?'

He was pushing her towards the door.

'No!'

'What?'

He opened the door, pushed her through. I'd slipped out behind her and looked round at him.

'We don't serve scruffs in here!'

We stood on the pavement, the sun coming through a crack in the white sky, and Very seemed bewildered. She looked down at her clothes.

'Do I look weird or something?'

'Well . . .'

'He wouldn't serve me . . . I mean, look!' She pointed at the dark-red door with peeling paint. 'That place wouldn't serve me!'

'Let's just go, Very.' I pulled her by the arm.

'D'you think I look like a tramp?' she said, and stopped in the street, her hands out either side, looking down at herself.

'No,' I said. 'You look . . . unusual.'

'But this is what I like wearing.'

I'd said I thought she looked fine and maybe it was the wellingtons.

Very is thudding back up the stairs to the kitchen that smells of bacon and looks out through the triangle of roofs to the river. Next to it is the bathroom. The loo is behind the door and you have to stand in the bath to shut the door.

The phone rings.

'Will you get it?' shouts Very. 'I'm going to die if I don't piss right now.'

'Hello?'

'Hello, heartthrob. You'd be the love of my life, oh God, if only you had a cock!'

'What?'

'Verity?'

'No, I'm Cath, her sister.'

'Oh. Sorry! I'm Eddie.'

I shout up the stairs, 'It's Eddie!'

'Hello, Eddie,' she shouts down the stairs.

'She says, "Hello," she's in the loo.'

'Ask her if she's coming out, will you, sweetie?'

'Are you coming out?' I shout up the stairs.

'I'm not leaving you on your bony-oney-oh, you

know,' she says, as she comes down the stairs and takes the receiver.

'Bring her too!' says a little ant-voice from the receiver.

She looks at me, chewing the inside of her cheek.

'Well . . .'

I am nodding frantically.

'Take me, take me.'

'Yeah, well, come over and we'll see.'

'I'm not coming all the way over if you're not coming out. I don't love you THAT much!' says the ant-voice.

'OK, OK. Come over and we'll all go out.'

When Eddie arrives he says, 'My God, you didn't tell me she was still in nappies!' and slaps his cheek and looks me up and down with his mouth open.

Every surface of my skin blushes, even my hands blush, I stop breathing and hold my lips together and look at the floor.

'Oh sorry, sweetie,' he says, 'you're at the awkward age, and don't I just remember THAT! The worst years of my life!' He leans back and hits the air with his hand. He looks at Very with his hand back on his cheek. 'Well, what are we going to do? We'll have to disguise her. We could dress you up as a boy – that would be nice.'

Then he puts a finger to his lips and goes 'Mmm-mmm' and points to my breasts which are beginning to show through my T-shirt.

I blush again.

'Oh sorry, sweetie, can't help it! Right, OK. I'm going to shut up. Have you got a beer in the fridge? Of course not! Silly me. I'm off to get some!' and he skips down the stairs.

We walk down the steps into the club, the walls are changing colour and the air is vibrating, bodies below us are pressed together and jumping up and down towards the ceiling pushing and falling into each other.

'All right. IN!' says an enormous black man with a beard, and pushes all three of us into the crowd.

'That's Butcher,' Very shouts into my ear. 'Because he's butcher than anyone else!' She laughs into my ear and it hurts – the sound from the speakers is vibrating through my body.

A man on the stage is changing colour in the spotlights, red orange pink, he is strumming a guitar very fast and shouting at the same time into the microphone. 'NOOOOOO FUTURE NOOOOO FUTURE NOOOOO FUTURE.' His hair is slicked up into red points.

I feel her pulling on my arm. I have gone into a daze, mesmerised by the discordant sound and jostling people, tight and sweaty bodies pushing up against me. Very pulls me through the crowd to the bar. The floor is slippy with spilt drink. Eddie is ordering and talking to a tall skinhead in a white vest. He hands me a Pils and shouts, 'Here.'

Very shouts, 'This is Tracy,' in my ear.

Tracy looks at me through black-lined eyes with violet eyeshadow all the way round them. She has stuck a nappy safety-pin through her cheek and it is red and swollen where the pin went through. She has black lips. She looks at me with a so-what, blank expression to my smile. She is wearing a patent-leather miniskirt and a stringy jersey. She holds Very's elbow and shouts something into her ear.

Eddie tilts towards me and thrusts a brown bottle under my nose.

'Sniff!'

I sniff and the world becomes raw and electric, a rush of blood around my head makes me gasp and for a moment the club goes tartan and the sound disappears. I hold on to the bar ledge.

Very leans across me.

'For Christ's sake, Eddie, she's not old enough.'

Eddie leans into me and shouts into my ear, 'You're old enough for anything, aren't you!'

I touch the thundering atoms and let my mind be rippled by the underwater light.

Suddenly there is a crash behind us, and I am surprised to hear a dog barking. A table has been flung over and two men are standing in front of each other. One has a tattoo of a dragon on his arm. Even in the noise there is a strange quiet around them, like the air has turned cold. Quick as a flash he breaks a bottle on the bar and lunges at the other's face. Blood pours down the side of his eye and he grabs at the air.

The other begins to kick his legs – I can feel the dead thud.

Suddenly Butcher is standing between them. He has them both by the back of the neck, his grip must be painful because they bend over, their faces contorted. The crowd parts as he leads them to the steps. He drags them up, one in front, one behind, and throws them out on to the street through the black double doors. He wipes his hands on each other and straightens his bow tie.

I'm lying on the sofa watching as the rain dashes against the pane in gusts. I can hear the sound of cars swishing in the puddles and the clip-clip of high heels running along the pavement. The sky is bright white and glowering with rain. Eddie is snoring under blankets on the floor, and Very is next door sleeping with a strange man.

'She doesn't half pick them!' Eddie whispered as we crept up the narrow stairs last night after the club.

He has short hair and a nose flattened by somebody squished sideways on to his face. He has pock marks on his yellow skin and huge shoulders.

'I wouldn't even go for someone like that!' said Eddie from behind his hand and made his eyes travel full circle. 'He's an ogre! Oh my God!' he said, and put his hand over his mouth, and we both started giggling. 'We'll probably get gobbled up in the middle of the night! Tomorrow morning we'll just find Very's feet in the bed!'

'Is he staying the night?' I said, shocked.

'Oh sweetie,' said Eddie, 'you're so sweet.'

Eddie wakes up and looks grey-skinned.

'What's the time? Where are my glasses? Make us a cup of coffee, sweetie,' he says, sitting up. Oh Christ alive, my back. I can't even sit up! I suppose her next door with her fancy man hasn't stirred. Did all their stirring last night!' He makes a sneering face.

I don't know why he is cross with Very, but I seem to catch it from him and pass her closed door with a resentful determination not to make HER a cup of coffee. But standing next to the kettle, waiting for it to boil, I look through the triangular gap in the roofs and see the glistening river and the glowering sky over the faraway buildings heavy with rain, and decide to make her a cup. Then I think of that big head with the squashed nose on the pillow, emerging from the candy-striped sheets, and pour the granules back in the jar.

I carry the coffee downstairs. Eddie is dressed.

'Thanks.'

He slurps and spits it out.

'Oh God, that's hot! What are you trying to do, burn me to death!' He pulls on his shoes, rubs his head, does up the laces, slurps his coffee, curses and stretches and says, 'Tell that bitch I'll see her sometime,' and bangs down the stairs before I can say 'Shsh'.

He leaves a hole of silence in the room that pulls me back down the long grey corridors. The first day of lessons. I sit down next to the window. The rain beats against the glass.

I felt ashamed standing there on my first morning not being able to answer the questions.

'Stand up, dear,' she'd said. 'This is our new girl. Say your name, dear.'

I said it quietly.

'A bit louder.'

I said it again. There were titters.

'Bit louder.'

I said it louder and she jumped back in a pretend startle.

'Oh yes, I think we heard that!'

The class laughed.

They'd learnt it all in Third Form and I didn't know it. We'd done Benito Juarez and the Revolution. The window of that classroom had looked out on to two huge hills that changed colour with the time of day. In the afternoon they glowed orange with the warm light, then they turned pink when the sun set. In the evening they settled into blue shadows like big sleeping animals, and at night when the stars were out, they woke up and turned black.

But in the morning they were dark-blue with white cranes flying across the ribbed purple clouds, and Señora Gomez would tell us stories about what the moon told her daughter as she wove the blossoming countryside into her dress, and what the hummingbird said through his tears.

But they knew 1066.

'All that time at school and no proper history, dear?'

I thought it was history but it was *foreign* history.

And they knew Belgium and the capital, and I only knew Tierra del Fuego that means land of fire, and Popocatepetl, and how to spell Oaxaca, but that didn't count here.

We'd made angels out of gold-paper circles that you cut in half and twisted round your finger to make a cone, so they stood straight.

'No, dear, don't sit down – I haven't finished with you yet. Did I ask our new girl to sit down?'

'No, Sister,' the girls chimed.

She put her head on one side, and held her elbows under the little black cape of her habit.

'Now' – she turned to the class – 'that you're Lower Four and have joined the Middle School, I hope you haven't forgotten everything you learned in Junior School.'

'No, Sister.'

'What was the Shakespeare you read in Junior School, Henrietta?'

Henrietta Whitehouse stood up.

'*A Midsummer Night's Dream*, Sister.'

'Well, would you like to ask the new girl if she's read *A Midsummer Night's Dream*?'

She turned to me and lowered her eyes and without opening her mouth very much said, 'Have you read *A Midsummer Night's Dream*?'

I shook my head.

'Pardon, dear?' said Sister Felicity with her eyebrows raised and a sweet smile on her face.

'No, Sister, I haven't read it.'

'Well, come along, Lower Four, what else did you learn in Junior School?'

'Have you read *Great Expectations?*' piped a voice from the back row.

'No, I haven't.'

'What is the date of the Battle of Hastings?'

'I don't know.'

'What is the capital of Peru?'

'Lima.' Thank God I knew one.

'What is the capital of Belgium?'

'Have you read *Pride and Prejudice?*'

'Who composed *Così fan tutte?*'

All the while Sister Felicity watched with a sweet smile on her face, nodding at the questions and raising her eyebrows to see if I knew the answer.

But it wasn't any of that, the not knowing. It was that light I had to look away from, had to edge my eyes slowly down the side, look over the top of her veiled head, or the edge of her cheek, to avoid. I could just look at the mouth, lips pressed together, with that satisfied smile, I could see the nose. She held it up in the air and must have always had that bulb on the end, in her line of vision, as she looked through those eyes. And it wasn't what they looked like either – I could even say they were pretty, black eyelashes and brown irises. It was the light in them, the glint I didn't want to see.

Because I knew if I saw it, and knew it really shone with what I thought, I would hate her with a poison I could kill her with.

She wanted me to get it wrong.

She wanted me not to know, and if I didn't look, if I didn't catch its light, then I wouldn't know for sure. I could stand in front of my new classmates and not know the answers, and everyone would laugh because I was new and that was all right, and it wasn't because Sister Felicity wanted to make someone ashamed and scared on their first day, it was because she wanted to find out what they knew, and that was all right, that was all right.

I get up. I walk about the room. I decide to peek in on Very. She is lying alone splayed across the bed. Snoring. I open the curtains a crack to see the pear tree. I climb in beside her and smell the boxer's smell on the pillow. He must wear hair oil. Did he go away? I ask Very's hair. 'Yez, inne dark,' says Very from her dream and I imagine him rushing into the early morning rain.

Very's dream is deep like a moss-covered stone on a riverbed moving gently to and fro in the currents. I know her dreams are deep and ancient and underwater. That's why there's a terrapin in an aquarium on the mantelpiece, and nine eels in the bath.

Used to be.

Until we spent one and a quarter hours trying to coil four into two buckets and splosh five at a quick dash into the square kitchen sink so we could have a bath. And that's why Eddie put his hands up to his cheeks and screamed, 'Aagh!' and again, 'Aagh!' when he went to make a cup of coffee, until Very came to calm him down,

because he wasn't expecting to see their green-and-
black-striped slithery backs swimming and coiling in the
water under the cupboard where the coffee mugs are
kept.

'Just shut up about it, will you?'

'But if you have three things, it won't be so bad.'

'It will!'

'You've only got a few days, though, Cat . . .'

'I know!' I shout, and bang my elbows on the yellow
table, spill the tea and hurt my elbow bones.

'I bloody bloody know that, bloody hell!' I press my
cheeks on to my fists so I feel my bottom teeth. 'Don't
bloody tell me that!'

But as soon as my anger goes away I feel like crying.

The day after the day after tomorrow I'm going back
there and I can already feel the dread.

Very looks into her tea.

'Bloody hell, shit,' I say through my teeth.

Very leans across and says, 'Bloody hell, shit fuck!'

Then she leans across again and says, 'Bloody hell,
shit fuck wank!'

I look up, she's smiling.

'What does that one mean anyway?'

'What one?'

'Wank.'

'What?' she says, leaning towards me.

'Wank,' I say.

'What?' she says again.

I say, 'Wank!' and the woman in the hat looks up from her egg and chips.

Very is laughing into her hand. I kick her. She tries to speak through her laughing and the woman is looking at her now with pursed lips.

'Masturbate,' she says.

'Is that what it means?'

'No, I'm just saying the word 'cause I like it. Masturbate. It means chewing.'

'That's masticate.'

But Very is giggling into her tea.

'Does it mean masturbate, though?'

'Does it mean what?'

'Masturbate.'

Then I realise and kick her again.

The Italian man comes over with two plates of bacon, beans and bubble, and wipes the table.

'This your sister, Very?'

'Yeah,' says Very.

He throws the towel across his shoulder.

'Ay, Katerina.'

A small but wide lady, fitted tightly into a glossy dress with an apron over it, comes through from the kitchen.

'Who's this?' he says, nodding towards me.

'Issa family resemblance, innit,' says the woman, wiping her hands on her apron, her sleeves rolled up to her dimpled elbows. 'Easy tell.' She takes the towel from his shoulder and hits him with it.

'Come on a' do some work.' She turns to us smiling with round dimpled cheeks. 'He talk a long day and

24

never do nothin'.' She bursts into a huge laugh and sways back to the kitchen, turning at the counter to point at the blue-and-yellow picture.

'See you sister paintin', darlin'?'

I nod.

'Iss very nice.'

Car squeaks, sounds echo, the sun comes through the grids in a pattern of dots on the road and there is a whistling, the sound of an underwater whale and the echoing thunder of the wheels. Very's head in a blue shadow moves slowly across the surface under the window lit by a yellow light. We come out into the sunlight again. There is the hammering of a road drill and yellow signs, and men in blue overalls shouting in foreign accents over the noise, and a caterpillar truck with an orange arm and a large claw, picking up earth from the drilled hole.

'What did you do?'

And we turn the corner out across the bridge, towards the blackened tower of Big Ben, the sun following us in bright ripples across the water, a long barge cutting through the light.

'I gave her a picture.'

Very looks at me and back at the Houses of Parliament and back at me, smiling. She is proud of them.

On the other side is a long white house with a verdigris roof and flagpoles with blue flags fluttering in the wind.

'What, a naughty picture or something?'

The bus veers round and we lean against each other and see black figures on plinths, one even standing next to a big chair, and more tall buildings.

'No, it was a picture of Jesus.'

'Why did you give it to her?'

She looks out the side window then up the street.

'Actually, let's get out here.'

And we walk down the aisle of the bus as it is moving and clamber down the stairs as it stops and on to the bright pavement.

'It was a present for her Feast Day.'

She stops in the street and turns round to look at me with her hands on her hips.

'You gave Sister what's-her-name a picture as a present and she told you that was a sin?'

'Yes . . . no . . . well, not exactly.'

'Fucking typical!'

And she starts walking fast with me running beside.

'But you don't understand.' I add quickly. 'It's pride, it's a capital sin . . .'

We stop.

'That's a new one . . . what the hell is a capital sin?'

'Capital sins are the sources from which all other sins take their rise.' I mumble the catechism into my jersey.

She shakes her head.

A black horse, sleek and restless, stands outside a sentry box under two lolling Union Jacks. Upon him sits a man with a red plume, and buttons that catch the light. He has a red jacket and a white sash and a gold helmet and a long drawn sword. His motionless face looks ahead.

'Oh no, I understand, Cath! I understand it's one of those nun head-fucks.'

She is speaking loudly and I am embarrassed in front of the people who stand looking at the soldier.

He has long white gloves, tall black boots and sits on a sheepskin rug.

'Are they always black, the horses?' I ask, trying to change the subject. He has silver armour and a cream fringe.

I'd given it to Sister Campion the day after the retreat. If only Natalie had written that word on my list maybe it wouldn't have happened. I'd painted it and outlined it with mapping pen.

A picture of Jesus with his hands out. I chose it because I'm very good at hands. His long garments were painted in folds and I had shaded each one so they really stood out. I was very happy with my shading.

I handed Sister the picture and stood waiting, looking at the picture and up at her face to see what she was seeing, to see whether she liked it. She took my hand and drew me close to the desk, she looked at me with her blue eyes and put her head on one side and closed her eyes as though she was thinking. She was still holding my hand.

'Now, dear.' She squeezed my hand and sighed. She opened her eyes.

'Now, dear, I want to say this kindly. I'm sure the other girls are very impressed with your drawing skills.' Her voice was soothing. 'But you are rather fond of praise, aren't you?' She patted my hand with her eyes shut. 'Rather too fond of your own achievement.'

'Too fond' had a cold emphasis that cracked her voice.

'Pride is a capital sin.'

Something hot came into my throat and heated my face up. I wanted to snatch away my trapped hand. It travelled behind my ribs and exploded in the V above my stomach and left a pain there.

We walk up the road and Very is walking fast. We reach Trafalgar Square. She shouts, 'Bollocks!' into the deafening noise of the traffic, and the buses and taxis thunder past as she grits her teeth into the choking wind of smelly dust.

We cross on to the immense square. Suddenly the huge lions, the soft sound of the water, the dizzying height of the column, and Very's shout are too much, and I hold on to the stone basin of the fountain and look at the water.

'Come on, we can sit down over there.'

The droplets are jumping up in little splashes.

Very pats my back.

'Come and feed the pigeons.'

The birds fly up as we walk through them, and past the fountains and the tall column.

'We can get some corn.'

'I think I'll just sit here for a minute,' I say, down on the bench.

Very looks at me for a moment, opens her mouth to say something then closes it and nods.

'OK, see you in a sec.'

I watch her walking off through the pigeons, the birds flying up all around her.

If Natalie had written pride on the list, I might have realised in time. I might not have had to feel as ashamed as I felt when I wobbled back to my desk.

We had to write on each other's lists, because that's what you do on retreats, listen to the voice. Sister Campion was taking us. A day of silent communion with God in the Middle School common room, in preparation for the 'real' retreat after half term. We'd sat in a circle. The long wooden tables pushed under the windows that looked over the red roofs and beyond to the hockey field.

I can see Sister Campion now, sitting there with her hands in her lap, waiting for us to become quiet. She never tells us to be. She waits for us to be. She is one of those nuns everyone wants to please, and me too. She smiles at us. She has blue eyes that look right at you, into you almost.

'Now, girls, this morning begins your conversation with God.'

Sister Campion doesn't talk about God like in the catechisms, she never talks about rules or special prayers or calls us by our second name. She never says and what is the right answer and makes you stand up to feel embarrassed that you don't know it. Every answer has a good point to it.

'Now how must we think of God? What do you think would be a good way to think of God, Tessa?'

'As a friend, Sister?'

'Oh Tessa, I'm so glad you said that. What a wonderful way to think of God.'

Everyone knows that this is the way Sister Campion thinks of God and there are some resentful looks in Tessa's direction.

'God is our friend,' says Sister Campion. 'He is our loving friend. And what does a good friend do, Pamela, say . . .' and she smiles a conspiratorial smile and bunches her shoulders and clasps her hands together with a twinkle in her eye, 'Say a friend of yours had a particular problem.' She leans forward and whispers. 'They might have BO,' and all the girls giggle and titter. BO is a big thing for us. 'Would you tell them? Would you find a way, as a kind and loving friend, to let them know their problem?'

Pamela blushes.

'Yes, Sister, I would tell them.'

Sister Campion looks at Pamela, nodding her head slowly and smiling.

'So would I,' she says, 'so would I.

'So we can imagine God as a kind and loving friend who will gently tell us our faults, who will care for us enough to bring every blemish and stain to our attention.

Because this is who God is, girls. God is love, God loves us so much he wants us with him in heaven. And he wants to make SURE we get there.'

'If he loves us so much why doesn't he just let us into heaven WITH all our sins?' says Eliza in a defiant voice.

A ripple goes round the common room – this amounts to blasphemy.

'I'm so glad you asked that, Eliza. What a wonderful question!'

And we are all impressed with Sister Campion for seeing it that way.

'God has given us free will. This is one of his greatest gifts! So WE have the power to choose heaven!'

A short silence falls. We listen to the clock ticking. Above the door Jesus is nailed to a cross with big wooden nails, and streams of wooden blood flow in rigid ribbons from his hands.

'Do you know the name for God's voice, in our minds, Laura?'

'Is it our conscience, Sister?'

'Yes!' says Sister Campion, clapping her hands. 'Well done!

'There is a voice inside your minds, girls. It will tell you when you have gone astray, when you have fallen short, when you could have done better. You will know. Today's retreat is a preparation for your three-day retreat after half term, and it is an opportunity to listen for this voice, girls, the voice within you, leading you to heaven.'

*　　*　　*

We stand up in silence and put the chairs back round the tables. The retreat has now begun.

We start enthusiastically to listen for the voice of God so we can report in our notebooks what we have heard and give them to Sister Campion for approval. We take to writing lists of all the things that 'are not as good as they could be' then swap them with 'loving friends', so they can add anything they think their friend should know.

I sit next to Natalie, so I swap with her. I was nervous at first – she's in French A, Latin A and Maths A and I'm in the Bs. But there is a shy kindness in her eyes as she pushes her list towards me.

Her list reads:

Don't study hard enough, could have got A for Virgil's translation
Not generous enough
Not honest
Tummy, thighs, hair
Lazy
Selfish
Greedy
Could be more helpful

I add 'Untidy desk'.

Natalie wrote on my list too but, with all the things the list said, it never said pride, and I wish it had. Then Sister Campion wouldn't have looked at me with the you've-disappointed-me look. She wouldn't have looked away from my drawing as she put it in her desk, not on top with the other girls' Feast Day presents, ignoring the folds I painted in varying shades. She wouldn't have looked up away from me and said, 'Henrietta, would you come and write on the board, please,' which meant I was dismissed and must go and sit down in my place with that feeling of shame in my throat.

Very is walking back through the fluttering pigeons. She sits down next to me on the bench and hands me the packet of corn. I open the packet. She looks all the way up to the top of the column. The plastic tears so all the corn slips down on to the ground, the pigeons gather, and flutter and peck around our feet.

'For God's sake, Cake-tin,' Very suddenly shouts, 'you're only human, everyone wants praise!'

She looks away beyond the stone lions. Very is frustrated because she thinks she can't explain.

But something was attached to the words. Some feeling came through her eyes and into mine when she said them and spread through me like a warm wind, and as we walk up the Charing Cross Road I feel it undoing me. And by the time we get to the small street that slips up the side by Leicester Square tube, past the rows of glazed ducks with flavours of soup and noodles in the air, past the rows of multicoloured paper flowers, and furry birds with feather tails, and every size of parasol, I feel a quiet breathing space in my throat where a sad voice had been singing on a minor note.

All the men in the street are Chinese. We pass a red dragon glowing in the window of a basement.

We're going up to Berwick Street, Very says, because she wants to show me Soho. But first we're going to meet Big Terry.

'So this is your sister, is it, Verity?' says a man with greased-back sandy hair and a jacket made of leather. We're standing in a dim interior, underground. On the bar are lights with orange lampshades and orange bulbs.

Big Terry was a burglar, Very says. Now he has a club in Soho. The club is smoky, with black-haired men playing cards in the back room with piles of real money and talking loudly in a foreign language.

'What d'you want?' says Big Terry, winking at Very. 'You can have anything you wish for!

'But we thought it was a joke really.' He turns to his friend beside him. 'Even though they pinched my new telly, and that's what he said, he said, "Terry, it's been that many years you've been doing it, it's a laugh you get it done to you!" He was right, I had to laugh! So I did, stood there and had a right good laugh . . .

'What does your sister want, Verity?' he says, turning to Very but looking me up and down.

I say, 'Coke,' to Very.

'How old's your sister, Verity?'

I creep behind Very.

'Thirteen.'

He turns to his friend and gives him one of those looks that means he knows a secret joke.

'Can we go?' I whisper to Very.

'They're all right, Cath, they're only being silly.'

But I don't like them. I can hear him saying, 'George's girl, that one,' and the other one saying, 'Likes them young, don't he!' and they both laugh.

'See the fight then, Verity – did he take you? . . . Into boxing, this one,' he says, turning to his friend.

Very nods and shrugs her shoulders. They both shake their heads.

'Yeah, he got beat, though, didn't he? Poor show! . . . She likes Dave Boy Green.' He turns to his friend. 'Don't you?'

Very nods.

'Hopeless boxer, though!' he says. 'Beg your pardon and all that.'

Very shrugs.

'He missed a lot of training, he had an injury.'

Big Terry gives a knowing wink to his friend.

'Training. Did old George put a bet on for you?'

Very shakes her head.

'For himself.'

'Bet he lost a fair amount!' he says, swiping his head with satisfaction.

Very nods, shrugs and smiles. I sip my Coke between holding my breath, nervous of the club, the smoke, the men in the back and the two wide-shouldered men standing at the bar.

We walk out into the surprisingly bright day after the

subterranean darkness and into the hubbub of China-town. There is a smell of duck being cooked in the restaurant above Big Terry's black entrance. From the outside you wouldn't know there was a club there.

'That's the point!' says Very.

Who's Old George? I ask.

But Very doesn't answer every question.

We cross Shaftesbury Avenue and walk up Frith Street. We look in the window of the shop on the corner and look at the white-and-blue cooks' trousers that Very says are good for painting in. I wonder why she needs any clothes for painting in when all her clothes have paint on them. We walk along Old Compton Street and look at the strawberry tarts in Pâtisserie Valérie. Up past the market stalls selling pyramids of oranges and apples on green grass cloths and by the Raymond Revue Bar with photographs of women wearing costumes made of feathers that don't cover anything, in framed glass cases that light up, on display outside. In Berwick Street there is a good butcher, says Very. We stop at the good butcher.

'What shall we get?'

Neither of us has any idea how to cook.

'Look at that tongue!' says Very in disgust. 'It's a whole tongue!' And there on a square silver dish is the whole dismembered tongue, its roots and all the taste-buds.

'Lets get that.'

I watch from outside as the tongue is scooped off the plate and into a bag. Very comes out of the shop looking satisfied.

'How will we cook it?'

Very shrugs.

'I don't have a clue. Boil it, I suppose.'

'Aren't you supposed to skin it first?'

'I don't like thinking about it,' says Very. 'It makes me think of my own tongue.'

So we go home and boil it and it makes more and more froth like saliva. It is probably cooked but it looks just the same as a big pink tongue looks when it's still in someone's or a cow's mouth so neither of us can bring ourself even to touch it, far less taste it and have it touch our own tongues.

'What d'you want to do, go for a walk? I'll show you Brompton Cemetery. It's nice there.'

Very is in her vest and pants. She is seventeen but still it's vest and pants. She doesn't like her legs, they are long and muscular, 'footballer's legs' she calls them. Sometimes we get in the same bath, feet to head like two fishes squeezed in a broiler. We lie in the warm water with no intention of washing as though we are being cooked.

She says, 'Will you swap legs? I like yours better.'

'OK,' I say, 'these are your legs from now on.'

She is hopping about looking for her plimsoles. I am lying in my bed on the sofa. The windows look out on to the garden in the middle of the square. I don't have to get up, I don't have to go down to the refectory, I don't have to say good morning to Mother Agatha or go to devotions, or benediction, or say the Angelus at six o'clock or the De Profundis after lights out.

'D'you think I can wear this with this?' She holds up some creased blue trousers and a stripy jersey with holes in the elbows.

'Why don't you wear the green jersey – it doesn't have those holes.'

She sighs and pulls out the green jersey from the chest under the mirror.

'And that kind of greenish skirt you've got.'

She looks around for it. I am under the covers watching her from my warmth.

She shrugs.

'I can't wear that.'

'Why?'

'I can't remember where I've put it.'

'I hung it up next door,' I say. 'It was lying on the bathroom floor.'

'I don't really like it, though,' she says, screwing her lips up.

'Well, they're my legs, remember, so I get to say what they wear.' Her smile glimmers through her straggly hair.

She goes next door to fetch it. She puts it on under the green jersey and looks in the mirror with her head on one side.

'Yeah, that's all right.'

And turns to me, smiles and jumps on to the sofa.

Then pulls off the duvet and climbs in beside me with her shoes on and lies still.

'What are you thinking about, Cathy?'

'I'm glad to be here, I'm so bloody glad to be here and not there.'

'Only a few more years, small fry, and then you'll be free.' She has green eyes, I am silent.

'Now I'm going to tell YOU what to wear!'

We walk along the King's Road. I am wearing a pair of Very's grey corduroy bondage trousers with leather belt loops and straps between the legs and a zip that undoes all the way round so the legs come apart, but she's allowed me to choose my own jersey.

It is a bright autumn day and the pavement is patterned with long red leaves, pink on the underside. The cars zoom along the King's Road and we cross over and walk down Elm Park Gardens and the leaves on the pavement are small, pointed and yellow.

People are sitting outside the Italian café in the Fulham Road and talking in Spanish. And I wonder if Very ever thinks of the blue trees that dropped their petals in the road, or the sunlit red house and the dark kitchen that smelt of chillies and chocolate, or the silver arms and legs that clicked together in the breeze.

Outside the gates of the cemetery is a bus stop in front of the betting shop. A portly Chinese man is standing waiting for a bus. As we pass by he touches Very on the shoulder. He is smiling, she looks at him and smiles, he speaks in a foreign language.

Very nods.

'Good morning,' she says.

He takes a large wad of notes from his pocket. He is smiling and nodding.

'Oh did you just win that at the betting shop?' says Very. 'Yes? Well done!' She is smiling and nodding, pleased for his good luck.

He points at me and then at her, smiling and nodding himself.

Very says, 'Yes, I'm so glad for you, good morning,' and we both walk along into the cemetery.

To our disquiet he stops waiting for the bus and follows us into the cemetery with his wad of notes in his hands. Very and I look round and begin to walk a little bit faster. He walks faster behind us, and follows us as we turn left between the trees and gravestones. Eventually we begin to run but he is running behind us.

'He's got the wrong idea,' says Very, breathless, and stops running.

He is looking upset. He has a big face and it is creased across the forehead like the red Chinese lion at the V & A. We are in the middle of the cemetery between the yew trees.

She turns to him.

'NO!' she says to him. 'Sorry! Misunderstanding, misunderstanding!' She takes my hand and puts it under her arm and shakes her head again. 'No money, no!'

He lifts his shoulders and drops them abruptly letting out a short sharp burst of air through his lion nostrils, but turns on his heel and walks back towards the gate.

Very and I watch until he has disappeared, then look at each other. We are both a bit shaky.

Very scratches the side of her cheek.

'Got that one wrong, didn't I, Cathy?' And then begins laughing.

We walk around the cemetery reading the inscriptions and laugh at the Colonel's pile of cannon balls.

We walk back out through the cemetery gates and it begins to rain. We hoist our coats over our heads and walk towards the river. The raindrops make expanding circles in the puddles and the pavement reflects the sky so we walk in the treetops. The cars slide through the wet air like sharks.

By the river the air is clear, washed clean of dust by the rain, and the water is pale-blue. We talk about nuns, boxing, and men being gay.

By the time we reach Old Church Street we are on to God.

'But it says we're made in his image.'

'Do I look like a man with a long white beard?' says Very, stopping on the pavement and looking down at herself.

'No, but . . .'

'He's made in the image of the men who made him up!'

'Is man a mistake of God's or God a mistake of man's?' she says in her quoting voice.

'Don't you believe it then?'

She shrugs.

A jigsaw comes apart under my feet and I feel I will fall through it.

'Don't you even think God is holy?'

'Arse-holy!' she says.

We turn down a street past a row of people dressed in leather and straps and stockings. Except for a young woman in a neat suit. As we walk past the young woman begins to sing in a high trilly voice, ' "Touch-a touch-a touch-a touch me, I wanna be dirty. / Thrill me, chill me, fulfil me, / Creature of the night." '

I look at Very to see if she finds this odd but she is striding past hardly noticing them.

I am mesmerised by this strange line of people standing, some in suspenders on such a cold day, men with mascara and eyeliner and dyed black hair and lipstick, men in lipstick, but Very doesn't bat an eyelid. As I pass, a tall man flicks open a silver lighter and stands looking at the blue flame. A bald man with a deep voice, three people behind him, sings, ' "There's a light," ' and someone joins in, ' "Shining in the darkness," ' while the girl up the line sings, ' "Touch-a touch-a touch-a touch me," ' and it sounds pretty.

'Very, who are those people?'

'Religion is the opium of the people.'

'The what people?' I say, running to catch her up.

'Opium of the people.'

'Those?'

'No, religion is.'

But I don't want her to tell me any more about that.

'Did you ever take that, opium?'

'Yes, but it gave me a bad dream.'

'Why do "the people" want a bad dream?'

'Those people? No, they're waiting for *The Rocky*

42

Horror Show. They always dress like that. Are you hungry?'

When we get back Tracy is shivering on the doorstep.

'I'm bloody soaked, Very!'

She's wearing an obscene T-shirt of Snow White and the seven dwarfs, the patent miniskirt and big boots with buckles that chink when she climbs the stairs.

She ignores me and talks to Very.

'Anyway, yeah, I said 'e couldn't take it for nothin', but I let 'im borra it.'

Very says Tracy fakes her accent to sound hard. Very said I need a few lessons in sounding hard so I can say 'Fuck off' to men like the one who tried to chat me up in the café. She said I'd have been walking off down the street with him if she hadn't been there to save me, just because I couldn't say 'Fuck off', which is the right thing to say to a man with greased-back hair who keeps tilting his head to the side so he can look down the full length of you without the table in the way. You just say 'Fuck off', just like that, quite quickly like Very did when she came back with the mugs of tea. He got up straightaway and walked past the glass window swearing, and gave her a dirty look. You're not supposed to worry if they do that, though. You just have to ignore the whole thing, say it quickly, that gets rid of them.

I don't think Tracy would have any trouble. She'd say it between chews of her gum, probably spit right at him. Like she did at Eddie when he called her a slag.

She has thick black slanting lines round her eyes today so she looks like an Egyptian. I'm glad her safety-pin hole has gone down. Very says she'll take me to see the Egyptians at the British Museum before I go back.

We light the gas-heater, both bars. We take our coats off and hang them on the back of the chairs so they steam and the room smells of wet wool. They steam up the windows. Very goes to make tea. I lie in front of the fire trying to get warm.

The rain turns to hail. It rattles down the chimney and bounces on to the hearth through the gap Very made when she pulled the heater out to rescue a pigeon.

I've taken my wet shoes off but Tracy hasn't taken off her big boots.

She says, 'Are you a good convent girl? Do you say your prayers?' and plays hopscotch over my stomach starting at the feet.

I think she is going to stamp on me. Both boots to the side, both feet apart, she's reached my arms. She jumps to the side of my head, then feet apart over my face. She is not wearing knickers. She jumps to the side. I get up quickly. She gives me a sideways smile.

Very clomps down the stairs with a tray. She is proud. She has brought biscuits.

'Very?'

'Yes?'

'What about invisible things?'

'What about them?'

44

'Well, they exist, don't they?'

'How should I know?'

'But they're not the opium of the people, are they?'

'What are you talking about?'

'D'you ever see things that aren't there?'

'Hallucinations?'

'Yes . . . are they?'

'Like if you take acid?'

'Acid? Did you take it? What did you see?'

'Thousands of multicoloured umbrellas.'

I look at the crack in the curtain where a chink of light comes through, orange-yellow light from the street lamp, and see spinning geometric shapes changing colour in the air.

We get off the bus at Charing Cross Station and the night is black and blue with clear edges, the rain has washed the air clean and the lights sparkle. I feel like there are sparks in the air that buzz and pop near my eyes. Eddie and Tracy are waiting in the queue under the arches. The lights flash on the walls and the beat of the music thuds into the night air but not the singing.

'Have you got your membership? I've lost mine!' says Eddie to Very, searching in the back pockets of his black jeans. He has a T-shirt with the arms cut off and his biceps move about.

'Oh but you've got goose-bumps to take in,' he says, nodding his head at me.

The night is cold in the queue and I feel hot crimson

coming over my cheeks. I look down at my breasts to see if they really do show. I try and cover them with my folded arms. The queue moves down the steps.

A man with chains in his ears and a black string vest that shows his fat muscles is standing at the bottom of the stairs.

'Gary!' shouts Eddie, 'I've lost my fucking membership!'

Gary motions him in with his head.

Very shows her membership to Gary and draws me in behind her.

'I'm taking her in!' she shouts.

'How old is she?' says Gary, looking me up and down. 'Looks about ten!'

'Sixteen!' shouts Very.

'Yeah,' says Gary, 'that's too fucking young anyway!'

Very looks dismayed.

'Go on, get in!' He motions with his thumb.

We walk along a red corridor and Very pays a girl with black eyeshadow, The music is so loud you can only mouth. Very holds up two fingers and says 'OO'. The woman says something with an 'AY' in the middle. Very's mouth makes 'WOH'. The woman's mouth says 'AYT', with a question mark in her eyes. Very nods. She points to the door behind us. Very pulls me through. The music is dulled a fraction. Eddie is already there.

'No! size nine, these are fives, for God's sake.'

There are two men behind the counter handing out roller skates and people in not much clothing sitting on the benches round the edge of a small room. Most people take their skates and go through another door, which lets in blasts of Earth, Wind and Fire whenever it opens.

We put our skates on and go through the door into 'Burnin', burnin', disco inferno', flashing lights and people in shorts and glistening legs rushing past on skates. Some really dance as they whoosh by, skating backwards, doing pirouettes and wiggling.

On either side of the stage are two men, one in sunglasses, doing leaps, hip rotations and back flips, all on roller skates and in time to the thudding music. The excitement in the air is so intense that I can hardly breathe.

Eddie seems to know everyone and is swept away into a crowd of men in tight T-shirts, all curling and half-circling as easy as they'd be on feet.

I feel unsteady. But there are plenty of square pillars to hold on to if your legs begin to splay out. The speed of the skaters is scary. They all skate round in one direction. The walls are shimmering with thousands of dots of light reflected off the spinning metal globes.

There is a balcony round the top where people are sitting drinking and watching and occasionally mouthing at each other. Very makes a drinking motion with her hand. I mouth 'Coke'. She skates off to the bar without difficulty and I cling to the square pillar, taking a little slip now and then.

Suddenly I'm pushed forward from behind. Someone is holding me under the arms and pushing me into the circuit. That's why Very got annoyed with Tracy. That's why she shouted herself hoarse even though you couldn't hear a thing. They'd screamed at each other up the thudding stairs and out into the quiet night we couldn't hear was quiet because of the leftover booming in our ear drums. All because of that.

She'd pushed from behind. Into the ladies' toilet. The doors were glassy red with a gap you could look under. The loo was black with a red lid, Tracy had dark-red nails, and she'd undone a packet of silver foil, and chopped some white powder into a line on the cistern, she'd rolled up a fiver and shown me how to sniff it up through my nostril, quickly, as though I was swallowing, and the chemical flavours had trickled down the back of my nose, numbing my throat.

My eyes had shot open wide then. My heart had started beating so fast I thought it was going to pop out of my chest. The next minute I was skating round the rink with all the rhythms in my body beating in time with 'She's got it, oh baby, she's got it'.

I'd run flat up against the wall, and got up, smack into a square pillar, and got up, skidded in a pool of lager, and fallen over again and again. But I hadn't felt a thing, only the thundering music and the wind cooling my sweat-soaked body blinking away the water that ran into my eyes.

'She's only fucking thirteen!' she'd shouted across the street.

So we walked to Trafalgar Square and Tracy walked up St Martin's Lane and they didn't say goodbye or goodnight.

'Why didn't you say no?' she said just before she stood stock still on the pavement and searched through all her pockets.

'I didn't know I was supposed to.'

But Very had that 'Oh fuck' look on her face, and started looking in the pockets she'd already looked in.

'It's been nicked!'

That's why we're walking down a great wide road to Buckingham Palace. Very says we might as well do sightseeing with the way things have turned out. She'd asked the conductor on the N22 if we could travel free, but he'd said, 'What d'you think this is, a bleedin' charity shop?'

She'd asked a woman in the queue if she could spare us the fare, and she said in an apologetic voice, 'I ain't made o' money, luv.' But when the man with black-rimmed glasses had put his flat palm in the middle of her back, pressed just a little and said, 'I'll pay for you, darlin,' she decided it was time for us to walk home, even if it was three o'clock in the morning.

An orchestra of booming sound fills my ears where the music has been. The booming space fills the wide empty road and the night air is alive with wings and coiled tails. They hiss and seethe under the road. And disappear out of and into the darkness of shadowed alleyways.

I can't stop talking and I ask Very if she realises that under the ground is a configuration of circles that bisect and trisect, inside a huge thirty-pointed star made of six pentagrams that carry forces that hold the city in a dynamic geometry, of points and angles and circular motions that keep it vibrant and rush with a speed that drives hidden stories out into the air. And she says she doesn't know what they're cutting speed with these days.

But I know that you can't stay still in this city or you'll be mown down by the force of it. You have to move like sliding along the top of a wave or you'll be plunged into its underdepths and crashed around among the stones. And the people who are walking and talking to themselves are walking and talking on the bottom of this sea. Or they have met one of the creatures face to face and it has spun their head in a million directions too real for their mind. For the winged beings are ancient and their memories are filled with too many visions for the small mind of a person. So they jabber and mumble and everything they say is true. That's why their eyes are staring.

I chatter on past the Palace and the quiet fountain, up the wide road, the trees shivering over the wall, past the black angel driving a chariot high above us, with its huge wings spread out against the sky, and on past the sleeping park.

Very nods and agrees and guides me across pavements and pulls my sleeve to avoid puddles while I share my incessant revelations. They begin to slow down and down, so that by the time we are home and up the stairs and Very is asleep and I am lying in my bed I have reached a deep-down hollow place filled with creeping shivers. I cannot sleep or shut my eyes, my jaw aches, my tongue tastes bitter. I get out of bed to look at the deserted street. A tin can is rolled along by an empty wind, the red light turns to green even though there are no cars.

I get back under the covers and fall into a disturbed dream where I wait for the red light to change outside Mother Agatha's office. It turns green. I wake up with a start. I must go in, I must go in the office, I don't know what I've done. Its all right. I'm here, not there. I look out at the street-lit sky. A car, the lovely hum of a car engine in the empty street, but I fall back into it and I'm in her office and she's saying about Tessa and I'm trying to wake myself up but this isn't a dream, it's a memory, and I'm trying not to look at her. I'm looking at the floor.

'Tessa Taite has told me something about you . . . It is polite to look at people when they are talking to you.'

But I am afraid of those cold eyes.

'I know you are new so I am prepared to be lenient.'

I don't know what I am being accused of.

'Tessa Taite says you have been cheating!'

I look at her eyes now. I am startled, my blood turns cold, I feel a trembling in my breath. Tessa is my friend, my own classmate. This must be a mistake.

'No,' I quiver, 'I don't think so.'

'You don't think so. Either you have or you haven't.'

I stand with my mouth open, helpless, I wasn't sure. With Señora Gomez it hadn't been like this. There were no tests, no competitions. We copied from each other's books and read each other's poems aloud.

Mother Agatha's face looks as if it has been scoured

with a Brillo pad – it is red with hundreds of tiny veins. She holds her hands in two fists, and even when she opens them they curl around like claws. I wonder what she calls cheating.

'I don't know, maybe I've copied something. Henrietta Whitehouse let me copy her Latin declensions. Maybe that was cheating.'

' "Maybe" is no good, dear. Either you're a cheat or you're not.'

'I'm not a cheat,' I say.

'Then is Tessa Taite a liar?' asks Mother Agatha in a chillingly soft tone.

Her face grows hard, her voice too.

'Or are YOU?'

'No,' I stammer, 'no, I'm not lying, no. I'm sure Tessa isn't a liar either. I don't know what's happened.' My voice cracks and I close my mouth and try to swallow.

It is all dark-brown, dark-brown cardigan, dark-brown buttons, dark-brown skirt, dark-brown socks. The blazer was folded last on the top with the hockey stick and we sat on the lid it to make it close.

'Well, as you are a new girl and you're joining a class of girls who know one another very very well I will let it go this time. But let this be a warning. These things do not go unnoticed, and . . .' she says, and leans forward entwining her clawlike hands together, 'there is a saying: "Give a dog a bad name and hang it!" '

I walk down the cold corridor away from her office and back into the London night.

I get up and go into Very's room and the light from a

grey dawn comes through a crack in the curtain. I look out on to the garden and the pear tree. I climb in beside Very. I lie next to her and breathe in the light of her luminous dream. A small being, thin as a crescent moon, steps out of the bottomless night, and into my mind, and I fall asleep.

'Look, it's eleven-thirty!' says Very, holding the clock next to my face. She is dressed and the curtains are open. I am so glad it's not last night.

'I brought you a cup of tea,' she says, pointing to the table, 'but it's probably cold by now!'

I am so glad to see her, so glad the night is over, even though my whole body aches and when I get dressed I see my thighs and elbows are covered in purple and yellow bruises.

It's only when we open the front door and smell the autumn and feel the strangeness in the air that I see in my mind a wooden door with an iron handle in a red-brick arch and my stomach turns over. Very has seen it too.

'Come on, you're here now, you can't spend your whole time dreading it.' She takes my hand.

It's like getting ready to die.

It is breezy. We cross the King's Road and walk along past Mrs Turpin's Art Store. She has a son called Dick. Like the Highwayman.

'How will we get there?'

'We're going to take the 19 bus.'

'But it's going the other way, Very.'

She looks at me, puts her arm round my shoulders and squeezes.

'Don't worry, Catkin, the buses go both ways!'

'How do you know which way to go?' I say weakly.

'Because it says on the front.'

'How did you find out all this?'

She stops – she is counting out our bus fare – and laughs.

'You just get to know. Now, have we got enough for both ways AND a piece of cake?'

We walk along under the trees and past the fire station.

In a doorway set back from the road an old man is sleeping. His face and hair look as if they are caked in white clay as though he has been dug up, his feet are wrapped in newspapers and tied in blue and orange string. Very walks over to him as though pulled by a magnet. She looks at him for a long time. Suddenly his eyes open and look straight at her, yellow eyes. She starts back then leans down and gives him all our bus fare. He picks it up from the neat pile she has left and throws it at her growling.

It scatters across the pavement, we hurriedly pick it up, and see the 19 approaching round the corner. We climb on and run up the winding stairs to sit on the front seat on the top deck and watch London pass by.

When we have wound around the leaping chariots and a field of tall trees swirling with falling leaves, Very telling me, 'That is Hyde Park Corner. This is Green Park,' she says, 'Maybe he just doesn't like charity.'

The sun has come out, the shadows of the clouds are scudding over the courtyard of a gigantic temple. We walk up the wide flat steps, through the tall sandstone columns and enter a shining marble hall that echoes our footsteps. We climb up the swirling green marble stairs.

I touch the smooth cold surface of the banisters. The air smells of stone. Up and up we walk.

We wander around the third millennium BC examining the bird goddesses with earrings and when we enter Ancient Sumer Very is delighted to find Lilith flanked by a cat, and an owl with two beautifully fashioned footballer's legs.

'I'm going to show you something – it's with the mummies.' She takes my hand.

'What?'

'The Egyptian mummies.'

'Sarcophagi?'

'Yes.'

I like those painted coffins.

But I don't like the dried-up body she shows me, in the bottom of the glass case, with long, dark-orange hair, curled around and sleeping for everyone to see.

'It's amazing, don't you think?' whispers Very.

I edge towards the doorway backwards, and breathe in quickly.

Very is getting out her sketch book to draw.

'No, Very, I . . .' A funny sound comes out of my mouth when I see a transparent child with big eyes standing in the corner by the empty glass case. 'Can we go?' I say with a kind of sob I don't mean to let out.

When it climbs inside the glass case and stares at me, I gulp, turn round and walk out. Very follows.

'Sorry, Cath, I didn't mean. . . sorry, listen, don't worry.'

We are walking down the stairs and tears are pouring down my face. We pass by some hacked statues of a woman with a lion's head but they all seem to be crying too, and I begin sobbing uncontrollably.

We reach the next landing and Very stops me, puts her arms round me and hugs.

'Don't cry, Cath, don't cry, I'm sorry, I . . . don't cry. It's OK.'

I calm down and wipe my nose on her shirtsleeve.

'It's OK, I feel better.'

'We'll go now, get some cake, OK?'

We walk through a huge hall following the 'Way Out' signs.

Back out on the steps, the evening is drawing in, the street lights are glimmering from pink to yellow and the cool air clears my mind. Very has her own face again and people are pulling their coat collars up against the wind.

The clouds are purple, and between them are strips of cobalt blue. We are walking along Great Russell Street under yellow street lights towards Soho and the cake shop. Very's shadow is turquoise on the pink pavement.

* * *

'Hello, mate, gotta pass, gotta pass,' he says, flashing it to the conductor.

'Lost my job, gave me a pass,' he says loudly to the woman next to him.

'Stacking boxes,' he says, nodding.

She looks uneasy and gets up.

'Stacking boxes,' he says to the man across the aisle. 'No jobs these days, yeah, stacking boxes. Gave me a pass.'

A tall thin-necked African sits beside him, with beautiful long fingers.

'D'you like hotels?'

Outside light streaks up the columns above the arches and illumines the smirk on the white marble faces of the Ritz, written in light bulbs.

The African man nods.

'I stay in Brighton with my wife, gotta wife? That's good.'

Green Park has gone black and when I look out the window I can only see the reflection of the opposite side of the street rushing past.

'You know you have to go back, Cat,' she'd said.

I have to look up close and through my own dark face to see the blackness under the trees.

'Can't eat lobsters, though, saw them being killed, didn't like it, cruel, never eat lobsters, felt sorry for them.'

We wind around Hyde Park to the buildings now illuminated by rows of oblong windows and past the yellow palace with square columns holding up a triangle of stone.

'I like watching Fulham, they don't muck about, like football?'

'Oh yeah? Madagascar.'

The buildings are lit by pink lights. Black mannequins pose in sunglasses and sequins that glitter as the bus sails past.

'Madagascar, yeah. Giant tortoises are big, aren't they?'

When we turn down the Fulham Road the sky is black and there's a waning yellow moon low in the sky.

PART TWO

I am standing outside the arched door with the round iron ring. The taxi brought me from the station and left me on the stone step. Very counted out the money. She gave it to me in the palm of my hand.

She said, 'That will be enough for the taxi.'

Eddie was crying.

He said, 'Oh I can't bear it! I can't bear it! I know what it's like being thirteen!'

But I didn't feel anything then.

Very had phoned up the proper night for going back and said, 'I'm so sorry, she's ill, I've put her to bed, yes, this is her sister Verity,' as though she was about twenty-five.

That voice made me cover my hands over my mouth and double over in embarrassment. Then when she put the phone down we'd both gone screaming round the room as though I'd never have to go back, as though she'd solved it for ever.

But in the end I'd had a day's reprieve, a day in Kensington Gardens in the sunlight feeding the swans, and we'd stood on the platform at King's Cross with Eddie crying his eyes out and Very doing up the buttons of my cardigan, which was ridiculous because when in her life has she ever bothered if somebody's cardigan was done up?

It didn't even hit me in the train. I just went along with the rhythm and it felt like a good rhythm, steady and endless. It lulled me and I didn't think of anything. I just never wanted the rhythm to end, that's all. Even in the taxi my mind wasn't awake. It was those trees. When I saw those trees at the end of the drive, the ones that shed bugs and beetles on to you, lime trees, that nothing grows under because they have poison in their roots, that's when it hit me. It began in my stomach like a worm squirming, and rose up to my throat so I could hardly breathe.

He turned round and drove off and I watched his red lights going down the curved drive under the poisonous trees.

I could go in now, I could turn the iron handle, but I can't keep my eyes off the spindle-berries. They are soft and pink, and inside the four slits are shining orange seeds.

We'd been to the French café where they had *chocolat chaud* and fresh croissants. We'd sat there for two hours, pretending we were foreign. Very had three coffees and couldn't stop talking, and crossed the road without looking. She nearly jumped out of her skin. The cab-driver shouted, 'Fuckin' mind out ya cunt,' and Very had stood stock still in the road blinking at the back of the car. I had to drag her to the other side. She kept saying, 'Honestly!'

I put down my bag. I turn the iron handle with both hands, and it creaks open. The locker room smells of wood and wet wool. The Upper School choir are practising in the concert hall. Their high voices singing threads of music into the air. They stop, I hear Mother Perpetua's reedy voice singing how it should be sung. They begin again. I walk up the grey steps towards the classrooms and along the corridor.

I open the door of Lower Four.

The girls are huddled round the desks by the radiator, all talking at once. No one looks round.

'Can you imagine, she gave it all up?'

'Just like that!'

'Who gave it all up?'

'She told Lower Five she cried for nights on end pleading with God to let her have her life in the world.'

'Who?'

'Sister Campion.'

'She didn't want her vocation?'

'No!'

'She was going to get married.'

'She had to be a bride of Christ.'

'Oh that's awful.'

'God, she must be holy.'

'When she was a novice she was riddled with doubt.'

'Yes, but when she took her final vows, it was like the calm after the storm, she told Lower Five.'

'It's because she followed God's wish for her instead of her own,' say two girls in unison.

'And every day she thanks God for her calling.'

'Oh God, please don't call me!'

I stand behind a chair and smooth the yellow wood, back and forth, back and forth.

'AND she had beautiful long golden hair!'

'Well, she must have had to have it all shaved off.'

'Yes, when she took the veil.'

'Is it all shaved?'

'Yeah, under their veils they're all skinheads.'

'No!'

'Well, how d'you think they get the veil on?'

'How do you know?'

'Once Juanita Fernandez climbed up the drainpipe and looked in the window when Sister Gobnet was undressing.'

'You're joking!'

'Yes, on to the flat roof above Blue D.'

'What did she see?'

'It's surprising Juanita Fernandez hasn't got expelled already with all the stuff she does.'

'I told you, she saw Gobby getting undressed.'

'She already did get expelled.'

'But what did she *exactly* see?'

'Well, how come she's still at the school?'

'She saw that her head was shaved and she was wearing . . .'

'Her father's rich, that's why, so he paid for her to get taken back.'

'LISTEN, I'm talking!'

'OK, we're listening.'

'She was wearing . . .'

'Can you do that? Pay not to get expelled?'

'TUT! Well, fine, if you don't want to know!'

'We do! We do want to know! Tell us what was she wearing!'

'OK, she was wearing a black bathing costume that covered her thighs, and buttoned up so that you had to undo it to go to the loo. They have to wear them in the bath because they're not allowed to look at their bodies – it's sinful.'

'Yuk, so they never get to wash properly?'

'Is it sinful for everyone?'

'But she'll get expelled now, won't she?'

'What she's done is sacrilege!'

'How do they wash, though?'

'Not if Sister Gertrude's going to get her new chemistry lab, she won't.'

'Listen, I've got a joke. What's the difference . . .?'

'Is he paying for the Upper School extension?'

'What's the difference between a nun praying . . .'

'How should I know – probably.'

'What's the difference between a nun praying and a nun in the bath?'

'One's got hope in her soul – everyone knows that one, Lucy.'

I go back out and close the door. If I hurry I can put my bag upstairs before the bell rings.

I walk quickly down the refectory passage and run up the creaking polished stairs to the dormitory.

'Slow down!' says a voice at the top. 'What are you doing on the landing at this time?'

'I came back late, sister,' I say breathlessly. 'I was ill, I had permission. My sister Verity rang up – I wasn't well.'

She holds up her hand.

I stop talking.

'Which dormitory do you sleep in?'

'Yellow D, Sister.'

'Well, the windows in the yellow dormitory are being repaired after an unfortunate incident. Some of you have been moved to Merton. There is a list on the dormitory door.'

I walk back downstairs to the dark locker room. The Upper School have finished choir practice. I put my blue bag with my home clothes into the locker and close the door, then open it again. I take out my rolled-up T-shirt and hold it. I stand in the dark locker room holding my T-shirt until the bell rings for first-wave supper.

I have a new head of table. Her name is Lavinia and she has a hooked nose.

She says, 'Don't sit there, that's Imelda's place,' then she smiles at me, but her eyes don't, they say, 'Get it, stupid.'

I have my tray and I don't know if the other places have been taken. The refectory is filled with cutlery sounds and talking, the smell of slightly burnt pizza, and washing-up liquid, which wafts through on hot winds from the dish-washing room.

'Well, sit down!'

'Is it all right if I sit here?'

'Is it all right if I sit here?' she mimics me.

I put my tray down as far away as I can from her seat.

Soon I am sitting among a crowd of Lower Fives, who I don't dare talk to. Lower Fours are lower than any of the others in the school except Third Form, and every-one thinks Juniors are sweet. You stop being sweet in Fourth Form and start growing in all directions. Like lambs when they start to bulge out and turn into sheep. They're not sweet any more either.

I hope they are going to talk about the 'unfortunate incident' but instead it's who got what in the test on the Black Death, which I don't want to think about along with burnt pizza.

I am contemplating the large slice of dry sponge dipped in apple, when to my surprise a Lower Five turns to me and says, 'It's as dry as a carpet!' pointing to her apple sponge.

I smile and nod and blurt out, 'D'you know what happened in Yellow D?'

Her eyes light up.

'Don't you know?'

I shake my head.

'Oh let me tell you,' she says, putting down her spoon.

It turns out that Juanita Fernandez threw the statue of the Virgin through the window of Yellow D so it broke the frame and on to the roof of the gym where she miraculously remained in one piece but dislodged some red roof-tiles which slid down and smashed at the feet of Father Finnigan, which was another miracle because a few seconds later and they'd have landed right on his head.

Another girl joins in and they are once again talking among themselves. I discover that Reverend Mother said she was willing to overlook the firebell but that this was not a prank, and Juanita Fernandez has been expelled for good.

I keep having to push Very out of my mind in case I cry into my apple sponge – it's hard enough to swallow as it is. You have to finish it all up, though. That's what old beak-nose is for, to make sure you do.

I lie in the darkness after lights out, listening to them breathing sleep and know that there is sometimes a good thing in a bad thing. No one wanted the window bed, because of the draught, they said. So I got it. The bed pushed into the alcove of three windows. I can pull the curtain over my chin, and my head is in the moonlight looking out at the night and the dark trees, upside down and shivering in the sky. And through the open crack I can smell the wind from the night. It has come from the river.

And if you walk that way, over the grass, through the trees where the yellow sycamore leaves are falling in heaps, through the saplings and the grassy wood and over the fence, you are out of bounds. And if you carry on down the hill, through the tall reeds where the mud sucks your feet, you reach the snaking river.

And there are gaps when they don't notice you're gone, sometimes only long enough to get halfway there, but sometimes you can. Sometimes there's enough time to get there. Right there, to the place. The place where it's hung over, with ivy and brambles. Where the dried-up yarrow stalks are twirling with bindweed. It is a place that has a quietness. A special kind. As though it is listening. And when you speak, it hears.

When you go there it's like being with Very. You know you're safe because something is listening. The way Very does. And that person who disappears sometimes can climb into your throat, can remember who she is again because the silent place is listening. And it's safe.

And if I pull back the curtain over my chin and look at the upside-down trees, I can think of the path through the rhododendrons and the sycamores, through the oak wood and down the hill, across the marshy grass and the reeds, and down to the overgrown place, the secret overhung place, where something listens. Then all of it is sort of all right, and I say thank you to Juanita Fernandez for throwing the Virgin through the window so it broke the frame.

Thank you, Juanita Fernandez.

The sky is still streaked with the before-sun streaks, the air is cold and frosty, you can see your breath and I forgot my gloves.

It was cold in the alcove getting out of bed. I tried to get dressed under the covers. I watched Pen brush her teeth in her pink quilted dressing gown in the warm side of the room. There was frost on the window when I sat up to put on my brown skirt. The sky behind the curtains was grey violet, but the yellow trees were glowing. The sun was still below the horizon.

We walk in pairs through the trees to the convent for

early Mass in the chapel. There is a nun behind us. In the file there is no talking. I walk with Natalie. She has long blonde hair and is the games captain's best friend.

We come out of the wood and walk up the path between low hedges towards the chapel and Reverend Mother's rose garden. We join the queue into chapel, a line of just-out-of-bed faces with sleepy eyes and heads draped in lace mantillas.

Natalie and the games captain have been separated by the move and when they meet they greet each other with looks of longing and excitement and clasp each other's hands and shake up and down whispering, 'I missed you! Oh I missed you! I can't stand it when you're not there!' Until Sister Clitherow glares and they bow their heads, but stealthily exchange notes to read in chapel, and we shuffle up the side aisles to take our places in the pews.

When we come back along the track through the yellow trees, the sun is up and glowing through them. It has melted the frost on the wet grass and is glowing through the yellow leaves.

Bellum, bellum, bellum, belli, bello, bello. Sister Scholastica still hasn't arrived. War, oh war! at war, of war, to war, by war. I'm standing in the store-cupboard queue revising my declensions before Latin behind a long line of Upper Sixes. They wear flesh-coloured tights and shoes with heels. They all have bosoms, and most wear crosses on gold chains that hide in the folds of their Upper School blouse. Nominative, vocative, accusative, genitive, dative, ablative. They stand absent-mindedly pulling the crosses back and forth along the chain, blinking slowly and looking elegantly bored.

I wonder if I'll ever be that grown-up. I stand Very beside them. She is like another species. I can't imagine any of them wearing wellies on the bus or eating candles.

Sister Scholastica comes hurrying along the corridor with the key to the store cupboard.

'Now then,' she says, passing in front of the Lower Six who are all taller than her and stand aside like grand ladies with their plucked eyebrows raised.

She opens her cupboard and bustles about among the piles of pink, yellow, buff and green exercise books, boxes of italic nibs of different thickness, rubbers, pencils, sharpeners, rulers, protractors, and blue and blue-black Quink Ink. The cupboard smells of new paper.

She sits inside, taking her time, checking each exercise book is full and marking it into her big ledger in beautiful italic script before she gives out a new one.

'There you are, dear, now let me mark that down.'

She has an amazingly monotonous voice. It can send you into a trance. She always speaks on one note. In chapel you can hear her singing because she never changes key. She sings the same loud note for every song.

Calligraphy is first lesson on Wednesday and Sister Scholastica teaches that as well as history. I like learning to make Ys with tails like ribbons, and curve the nib to make an O, and I have liked Sister Scholastica and her monotonous trance-inducing voice ever since she wholeheartedly admired my Q.

'That is a wonderful Q, Catherine,' she said. 'We'll have you writing italics in no time.'

I look round to see Olive standing beside me. She is looking out on to the yellow trees and I ask her if she thinks the sun is more yellow in autumn.

She says our sun is a yellow star, and some stars are orange or pink, and that planets in other solar systems are lit by different colours – imagine a red sun?

Olive is not in my half, she is in Remove. I only see her in the lunch or supper queue. I stand beside her and look where she's looking for a few minutes then ask her a question about the sun. Otherwise she just clams up. You can't ask Olive a direct question, like 'How are you?' or she just says 'Hmm' and something in her goes away from you. You have to stand beside her quietly for a few minutes and look out of the window at the swaying pine trees behind the chapel, and then say, 'No sign of the sun today.' Then she'll tell you that the reason the sun and the moon are the same size is that, although the sun is exactly four hundred times bigger than the moon, it is exactly four hundred times further away.

But today she's told me about the yellow star and I pluck up courage and ask her if she'll be my best friend.

She looks startled.

I feel my face go red. There is a pause. I look at the floor.

Then Olive says, 'I don't mind at all if you want to *tell* people that we are best friends.'

I say thank you, that will do.

'I mean it doesn't have to change anything.'

I say no, certainly not, things would stay exactly the same, it's just so I can say that we are.

She nods, so we agree to say we are best friends but for it not to change anything.

Olive wears pebble glasses but when she looks at the sky she puts her glasses on her forehead, so she can see. She has the distant vision of a hawk, she says.

I am standing in my goal-pads, the air is so cold my knees are mottled, and the wind blows up the back of my gym shorts. The rain which Miss Bolt says 'isn't rain, but just a drop of moisture in the air, Lower Four', is hitting my thighs and my face.

I watch Olive, a little stick figure in the far distance, walking slowly round the grounds. She doesn't do games. She has a problem with her blood or something so her heart can't beat too fast.

I wish I had a problem like that.

I jump up and down to get warm. The clack of the hockey sticks echoes from the other end of the field and I remember the wide blue sky, still and clear. And how the light rippled on the water.

We'd taken bread for the swans and one drew blood from Very's thumb. The sun reflected in a ribbon of light across the flat surface of the Round Pond and the swans drew V-shapes of glittering water through the ribbon of light. I watch the water in my mind, and feel the warmth shimmering on the surface.

Very's sketch book was filled with the curved necks and fluffed-out feathers of swans. They preened themselves in the sunlight, standing on one black rubber leg, coiling their heads backwards to burrow in behind their wings, the grass covered in discarded white feathers. And the coots dived and bobbed back up, making circles on the still water.

And I sat on the bench next to Very, listening to her charcoal scratching the looping necks, with the sun and the rippling water light on my eyelids, and I'd thought it would be a lovely thing to do: lie on the sunlit water with a breeze blowing through your feathers and your head on a long neck, burrowed backwards into your wings. Then the sky above the pond was filled with gliding seagulls circling and calling sea-sounds, and Very was hurrying to draw them, and every time she looked up the blue shadows of their spread-out wings would fly across her face.

Suddenly I see the mud-streaked thighs, and hockey sticks running full pelt towards me, the shining damp faces, the ball hurtling before them, and hear the breathing and the thudding boots. I try to clamber across into position in my unwieldy goal-pads but the ball is already in the net and the reds are cheering.

The games captain shouts, 'What were you doing? You weren't even in goal!'

My team look my way with contempt.

Miss Bolt blows the whistle and orders the players

back to the centre, then walks towards me, the whistle bobbing on a string around her neck. She has a page-boy haircut and big square glasses, like two television sets.

'You really do let yourself down, Catherine!' She wears pearlescent lipstick. 'But worse than that you let the team down!'

She crosses her arms and looks at me. She is wearing those stretch-nylon trousers with stirrups.

I follow them down to the mud.

'Sorry, Miss Bolt.'

'You really must learn to pull your weight a bit more!' she says, and stomps off to blow her whistle over 'sticks'.

It was a stolen day, the day we had in Kensington Gardens. We'd walked across fields of grass, and run through the trees till we were out of breath. Very likes the fountains when the sun shines. You can see rainbows in the spray. The clouds came and the rainbows vanished so we followed the edge of the Serpentine and sat down on a bench, and Very got out her book and read to me.

' "Anything which is against nature is a vice." '

I watched the ducks sitting on the green, wind-rippled water.

' "The most decadent type of man is the priest – he teaches against nature." '

I turned to look at her then.

'Did they write that?'

She showed me.

'Are they allowed to write things like that?'

I looked across the water at the seagulls, alighting on the other side.

The clouds were low, and heavy with rain.

' "You cannot reason with a priest . . ." '

A moorhen was standing in the shallows on one yellow leg. ' ". . . the only course is to imprison him." ' She laughed.

It began spitting. Very didn't notice – she was turning the page.

'We'd better get going, Very, look, it'll pelt.'

'Yeah, but listen –'

I was pulling her across the grass by her jersey to a place under a tall wide chestnut tree, where people were standing, while she carried on reading! ' ". . . the loathsome place where it hatched its monstrous eggs will be razed to the ground . . ." '

'Sshsh, Very, there are other people.' I was worried they'd arrest her or something.

She looked up.

'I'm only trying to help, Cath. Nietzsche wrote it, not me.'

The rain was pouring outside the canopy of leaves. The greylag geese were bathing. They dived forward and silver water slid over the feathers. They beat the water with their wings.

The whistle blows for end of games, and through the crisp cold air I hear another whistle blowing near the woods, and then another from lower pitch.

We walk across the grass in a drove with our woollen socks rolled down, mud-scraped knees, red thighs, hot and cold at the same time, red cheeks, glistening eyes and breathing out steam. We walk along the path through the trees to the hockey hut and the leaves are falling. The girls run to catch them, screaming, and every leaf is a wish and every wish is a 'he'.

There are circles of mud on the floor of the hockey hut where we hang our muddy boots. We change into our brown skirts in the cold locker room, our damp skin sticking to the wool and itching.

When it stopped raining, it started dripping under the chestnut tree. Very walked into the tunnel under the bridge and sang high notes to hear them amplified by the walls.

We walked through the wet grass, soaking our trousers, and between the tall avenue of trees. The band was playing in the cold wind and people wrapped in blankets were sitting in deck chairs while the thin brass-band music was blown away by the breeze. We sat down to listen in the deck chairs until a man with a green jacket came to tell us we had to pay, but I liked the sound of music in the distance as we walked away in the dying light.

We cut through the back streets, past tall white buildings, with big windows and creeping plants. The street lamps were turning pink and flickering to orange. The lights were going on inside the houses, and made the rooms inviting and warm-looking.

We held hands. I knew I was going back, but as the evening drew in everything was magic. Sometimes you step into them, moments when you feel as though the air is thin and another world hums beneath. You can feel it in your skin, and in the glowing colours, and then you know anything is possible.

And I'm glad Miss Tweedie told us about the atoms, twirling around each other in a magnetic pirouette, and that we are really made of space with lots of tiny dots shimmering and coming apart and spinning, that nothing is solid but full of space, empty singing space.

I am suddenly aware that there is a silence and everyone is staring at me.

Sister Felicity is looking at me with her arms folded, her head on one side, and her sickening smile, and I am in the classroom, sitting at my desk. I must have been staring out the window.

'Excuse me, Sister,' I say.

She raises her eyebrows, the smile unwavering.

To avoid the glint I unfocus my eyes, and start blinking rapidly to make the colours go away.

She mimics me with her head on one side, fluttering her eyelashes so the girls laugh.

'So do we have the privilege of your company in the classroom?'

'Yes, Sister.'

'Oh we are lucky!'

The girls titter.

But Piggy mutters, 'She was only looking out the window.'

'What was that, dear?'

'Nothing, Sister,' Piggy says quietly.

'Indeed.' Sister Felicity turns back to me.

'Be so kind as to repeat what I just said to Lower Four.' She puts her hand to her ear. 'And stand up, dear, so we can all hear.'

Perhaps Sister Felicity thinks her classes are fun. She has everyone laughing, and laughing is fun, isn't it?

I stand, I stutter, trying to remember if I caught anything. I wasn't paying attention.

'I'm afraid I don't know, Sister.'

She turns round and walks to the board. She has to stand on tiptoe to reach the top of the board with her pen.

She begins to write.

'Girls who pay attention do not need to . . .'

'Who can finish sentence?'

'Revise?' says Henhouse.

Sister Felicity looks around with her eyebrows raised.

'Fart,' mutters Eliza.

'Ask questions?'

'Ask stupid questions?'

'Come along, Lower Four, what word am I looking for?'

'Girls who pay attention do not need to . . .?'

There is a silence.

Sister Felicity is writing it on the board.

'Cheat! Lower Four! Do not need to cheat!'

'Now then, open your books at page two hundred and seventy.'

She means me. I'm the cheat. Does everyone know then? Not just Tessa who told on me? I can feel my face is red. I can't look up. Sister Felicity has left the offensive sentence on the board.

Natalie is standing up and saying a catechism. I look very fixedly at page two hundred and seventy. Natalie is sitting down.

'Well, Catherine, you have a chance to redeem yourself. Stand up, please.'

I stand up and look down.

'What is confession?'

'I . . . sorry, Sister, I . . .'

'She wasn't here, Sister,' says Piggy.

'Are you the new girl's *mouth*piece?'

'Well, she might not know we had to learn it, Sister. She missed doctrine on Monday,' Henhouse adds.

I sit down.

'How touching! TWO people to speak for you? Do you consider her unable to speak for herself? Well, perhaps you would like to answer the catechism for her as well?'

'Confession is to accuse ourselves of our sins,' says Piggy in a dry voice.

'To a priest,' whispers Henhouse.

'To a priest,' says Piggy out loud.

Sister Felicity nods.

'Well, Catherine, as you haven't learnt the catechism, you can read it. Can you read?' She looks at me once more, smiling.

I look past her veil to avoid her eyes, and there is Africa, big yellow Africa in a blue sea, with red pins stuck through it where the mission schools are.

'So . . . is sorrow for our sins because by them we have lost heaven and deserve hell sufficient when we go to confession?'

My voice wobbles as I read.

'Sorrow for our sins, because by them we have lost heaven and deserve hell, is sufficient when we go to confession.'

'Thank you, Catherine, that wasn't too difficult, now was it?'

'Cathy, quick, your sister's on the phone.'

I stand up and knock my chair over to get out of the classroom.

'It's Upper Five's phone time,' she calls after me. 'They said if I didn't find you in three minutes . . .'

I'm already running down the corridor, and past the biology lab to the phone box.

In the phone queue girls hand the receiver to each other and never put it down in case someone rings in between. There is only one phone box. No one can ever get through.

Lavinia, my table-head, is holding the phone and passes it to me with a sneer.

'Hurry up, Lower Four, this is *our* phone time!'

I close the door of the wooden box.

'Very? Very? Are you there?'

'Yes, Cath, I've been trying for ages.'

'I'm so glad you got through. Oh Very.'

'Can't talk long, Cath, I'm going to see Tracy – she's in a band! I'm going to see them practise. They want her to sing *lead*. Can you imagine Tracy singing!'

I want her to tell me about the terrapin, the rats, having tea in a warm room on a brown sofa, with furniture too big for the room, and a curtain rail that falls down whenever you try to close it.

'They're doing their first gig next week. Tracy says she'll put me on the guest list. I don't know where it is, a pub somewhere in Hoxton.'

I want to hear about the purple sky and the orange clouds, the hum of cars and the lights flickering on. I don't want to hear about Tracy.

Beak-nose is banging on the glass window, holding up two fingers for two minutes. I turn around in the phone box so I can't see her face.

'We spent the whole day tramping round North End Road looking for something glittery for her to wear. Eddie says she's just a show-off and she can't sing. She's shaved off all her hair! She's got a new boyfriend – he's from Glasgow called Brainy. Don't ask me why . . .'

As well as the wire that instantly connects our voices is another thin line. It speaks in the gaps, and the sound of someone breathing. It speaks in the silence. It has another language.

But Very hears it and says, 'Sorry, Cath, you don't want to hear about Tracy, do you?'

'Oh Very!'

'I know, you can't stand it there, but you'll be back here soon. Don't cry, Cath, it'll be OK.'

For one whole minute of my two left I cry down the phone.

Beak-nose is knocking on the window.

'I've got to go, Very.'

'Listen, Catkin, it's not long now, OK, and you'll be back here.'

'You put it down first, OK?'

'OK. Bye, Cath.'

I put down the phone and wipe the tears from my face on my dark-brown sleeve.

I walk along the corridor through the Upper School, and out of the glass door into the drizzle and the wind. I can say I'm doing an errand for Sister Ruth, because if they check Sister Ruth never remembers.

I walk through the tall pine trees looking about me. Nuns stand out like blots in the damp green. The raindrops hit my face.

When they say 'He cried out' in a book, they don't mean he shouted. They mean he opened his mouth and a long cry came out. It is pointed like an arrow's head and pierces the air. I have a cry like that in my throat. The feathers are in my stomach.

I run past the netball courts, along the edge of the hockey fields and into the wood where the trees are loud.

What I really want to do is lie spread-eagled on the ground, so my throat touches the earth, so the long line of pain is in the mud. I just imagine it would be a comfort. But I curl round on the dead leaves that are damp, curl around the pain and hold it to me till the wind dies down.

Very has records by people with strange names. Sugar and Fats, and Cream and Jam, but one tells you not to cry, not to cry, not to cry, and I sit under a tree with the leaves dripping, rocking back and forth, telling myself everything will be all right.

I thought the earth was yellow, like Mexico. Yellow ochre is earth. There's raw umber too which is dark-yellow, and burnt umber that is brown like choco-late, because the flames darken it. But Very says the earth can be red. Venetian red is the pigment, and it stains the brushes like Prussian blue. Then there's Mars violet.

But I never knew that the earth could be black, black like charcoal.

'No, dear, it's not black, its very dark-brown.'

The clay makes a glooping sound as Miss Sheldon prises it away from the roots it is clinging to.

'This is rich, fertile clay. That's why the grass is so green.'

We scoop the mounds she has dug into plastic bags, to carry back to the art hut.

The air is gentle, the sun is shining and the marsh echoes with birds. I don't want to go back to the art hut, I want to stay by the great slow moving river, under the black and yellow leaves, and make my clay sculpture here.

'Go and wash your hands in the river, dear,' says Miss Sheldon.

I have helped her to prise the sticky clay out of the earth and I am muddied up to my elbow; the grit is under my nails.

Miss Sheldon is wiping her forehead with the back of her hand because she has gloves on. Gloves for digging with a spade. She is an art teacher who doesn't like to get her hands dirty. I squat on my haunches next to the glooping hole.

'Rich and fertile – you can smell it!' says Miss Sheldon, sniffing the air.

Miss Sheldon always says things like that: 'rich and fertile', 'lovely and bright', 'pretty as a picture', words that go together in rhythms that you've always heard before. I wonder why she talks like that. She is always happy but her eyes are a bit bored. Not sorrowful, not anything, just dull.

I walk slowly through the trees, and the light is rippling on the water.

'Hurry along, dear,' she calls.

The trees are shedding yellow leaves into the water. I wash my hands slowly. They turn orange under the surface. The nettles grow on the bank and scent the air. I stay as long as I dare, gazing at the water light.

'Come along, girls, let's carry a bag each,' she says.

I want to climb up through the trees among the roots and the nettles, through the undergrowth and the brambles, I don't want to walk sedately along the path, in twos, and across the edge of the hockey field. I don't want to do that. I want to snake through the under-growth, I want to crawl down on my belly till I get to the bend in the river, I want to take off all my clothes and lie in the shallow water down there where the willow hangs over the river, I want the long green hair to touch my legs, I want to lie in the shallows, I want to dive to the bottom and touch the black mud. I want to come up gasping from the cold water, my hair in a long tail, with handfuls of mud and collect it in a great pile on the bank until there is enough to plaster all over me in streaks, till I am covered from head to foot, till you can't see my skin, only the mud-caked surface. I want to lie in the sun until I am dry and sit down in the wood in the grass and pine needles, and last year's acorn husks. I want to sit there and disappear into the earth, turn into the wood and wait until dusk.

We walk in twos back along the path that curves up the bank and through the trees and along the edge of the hockey field. Eliza and Pen stay close together when we walk along the edge of the pitch. They hold on to each other's jerseys, whispering and glancing at people from head to foot through slitty eyes, then looking away. This says 'We are saying nasty things about you'.

We walk behind the goal-net to the end between the rhododendrons and we can see the spire of the orange-brick chapel over the trees. We wind in among the bushes until we come to the art hut.

The art hut smells of creosote. Inside it is warm. There are benches all the way round under the windows, benches to sit at, and high stools. We spread them with boards and I take my dollop of clay and sit with it, black clay between my fingers. I can smell the edge of the river here in my hands. I roll it into a ball. Miss Sheldon is telling us how to roll it into long snakes to make a coil pot, but my piece of clay doesn't want to be a coil pot. It wants to be kneaded and pushed and smoothed out. It wants to have a face and arms and legs, it wants to have eyes to look at me and feet to walk along. It turns into a woman with long hair.

I give her hands and fingers and I put on a pair of ears but they don't look right so I take them off and imagine them under her hair. She is the woman who lives by the river under the roots. She is the one who swims at night among the long green hair in the water that strokes her as she swims. She is the one who dives into the black depths and feels the slither of the fishes.

Henhouse is standing next to me and giggling. Miss Sheldon is walking round inspecting our efforts. She comes across and looks at me and back at my clay piece. Henhouse is in stitches. I suddenly see my sculpture as they see her, a dumpy little being with long pointed bosoms and a huge bottom.

But on the way to tea, when we walk up the path to the locker room, Piggy and Hen walk beside me and ask if I want to do the history project with them.

'Yes, of course,' I say, delighted beyond belief.

'You do the drawing and we'll colour-in, OK? We'll start it in Saturday rec.'

'OK,' I say.

'She can do some colouring-in if she wants,' says Hen. 'They're my crayons.'

I thought it was Saturday wreck till Piggy told me what it stood for. We unroll the long piece of paper and begin in pencil to draw the history project. All the people are supposed to look as if they're walking round the class-room. Popes, kings on horseback and queens with veils.

The long tables in the common room are made of shiny orange wood. Hen's box of fifty brand-new co-loured pencils are arranged in a graded rainbow. We have to put them back in the right order. Sister Clither-ow usually reads us *The Lives of the Saints* but today she is unwell.

'OK, I've got one!' says Lucy.

'One what?'

'Life of a saint.'

'Belt up, Lucy.'

'What d'you want? Two breasts on a silver plate?'

'Not Saint Agatha!'

'What happened to her?' I ask.

'That was her martyrdom – she had her bosoms cut off!' says Lucy, pulling her jersey into two points and letting it go. 'And put on a plate.'

'Is that how she died! That's awful.'

'Oh I think she got raped first. They always get raped.'

'No they don't, they die defending their holy virgi-nity!'

'Edmund Campion, what happened to him?'

'Sister Clitherow, she's another one.'

'Another what?'

'Forty martyrs.'

'She had to lie with sharp rocks in her back and a door on top.'

'Mush under a door, tits on a plate . . .' says Lucy, holding out one hand then the other.

'Oh shut up, Lucy!'

'Hung, drawn and quartered.'

'Who?'

'Edmund Campion.'

'What does it mean, quartered?'

'Gutted.'

'When you're still alive, then they cut you into quarters.'

I look out the window. The trees are breathing the wind. The sunlight comes and goes. I make a path from the clouds, heavy with rain, to the rainbow of crayons, and the smooth, milk-white paper. I colour in the costume of the Cardinal and dissolve the colours with a paintbrush.

These stories are alive, folding and unfolding in the air. Very said the martyrs are sado-masochistic. I asked her what's that? But then Tracy said she'd tell me all about sado-masochism if I wanted and licked her top lip so slowly I decided I didn't want to know.

'What about Ethelburga?'

'She died of a tumour in her throat.'

'It was because of a necklace she wore when she was young. It was a punishment for vanity.'

'Natalie better watch out then.'

Someone sniggers.

'I thought that was Saint Lucy.'

'She died of her mortifications.'

'No, she had a sword piercing her throat.'

'That's Saint Agnes – Saint Lucy had her eyes torn out,' says Lucy proudly.

'D'you think any of them do mortifications now?'

'Sister Gertrude!' say two girls together, and then say, 'JINX!' and link their pinkies.

'I don't get mortifications. D'you go to heaven quicker, or what?' says Lucy.

I think of Tracy and wonder if piercing your cheek with a safety-pin counts.

Or burning a triangle on your leg the very same shape as an iron.

The Middle School common room has windows on three sides, but it is a dark room, with a dark-brown wooden floor, and a wall of dark-brown lockers. Everyone is knitting or working on their history project.

We're allowed to listen to a tape recorder. Fenella from Remove has a Stranglers tape and everyone is impressed. We are listening to, 'Golden brown, texture like sun,' and the song mixes with the sunlight shining in thin shafts through the small leaded panes in swirling dust beams, and the smell of wood-polish, and pencil shavings, and Hen's rainbow of colours in the glinting brand-new box.

*   *   *

I saw the triangle on Very's leg when we were getting undressed for the bath.

Her turquoise skirt fell on the floor. It's her only skirt. She still had her red socks on and her dirty white plimsolls with a black lace in one that didn't tie all the way up and left two holes empty. She stood there all bare except for her red socks and white shoes, and this purple triangular scab on her thigh, the shape of an iron, pointing to her knee cap.

I was already in the bath.

I drew my breath in, it gave me a shock.

'Bloody hell, Very, how did you do that?'

'It's just a burn,' she said.

'What d'you mean *just*, it looks terrible. You should have a plaster on it, a dressing or something.'

'It's OK,' she said.

'How did you do it?'

'Well . . .'

'How did you burn it that shape?'

She took off her socks and shoes and got into the bath and sat on the side on the flannels, and looked sideways down at the burn.

She looked at me then put her hand over her mouth and snorted, 'You'll never believe what I did.'

'What?'

'I was going out for dinner with old George and I had on my skirt.' She nodded at the crumpled turquoise on the floor. 'It's just I was about to go out and I saw it in the mirror, it was all creased, so I thought I'd better make an effort . . .'

'What? You didn't!'

'Nnn,' she said, nodding, without closing her lips because her mouth was smiling and she looks helpless when she's smiling like that.

'While you had it on?'

She nodded.

'You *ironed* it while you had it on!'

But Very was laughing, and I just lay in the bath shaking my head at her.

The sun goes in, the sky is grey above the trees, and heavy with clouds.

Imagine doing that! Putting the hot iron on your leg and not thinking. Very's got a screw loose.

'Why's it holy to be a virgin?'

'Oh shut up, Lucy!'

'It's not a joke, I'm not asking a joke, I'm asking a question.'

'Because it's sinful to you know what.'

'You know what what?'

'Belinda Pike's done it.'

'In Upper Five, Belinda Pike in Upper Five?'

'Sarah-Louise told Eliza.'

'But what is *it* exactly?' says Hen from our table, looking up from her colouring.

'What is what?'

'When they do it?'

'Don't you know?'

'She's only just twelve, you know, not everyone's thirteen!'

'But what do they do? Is it disgusting? Why doesn't anyone ever say?'

Piggy whispers in Hen's ear.

'Have I got one?'

Everyone laughs.

'Of course you have.'

'Doesn't she even know about the curse?'

'Of course I know about it!' says Hen, blushing.

'Well, where d'you think the blood comes out?'

'What blood?'

'See, she doesn't know.'

'She does so know.'

'I do!'

'Well, what d'you mean, "What blood?" '

'You bleed every month. Did you know that?'

'Yes.'

'No you didn't, you just said, "What blood?" '

'When you get your period you bleed every month.'

'Yes, I know,' says Henhouse in a strangled voice.

'And then he puts his *thing* in and that's called fornication!' says Lucy with a high-pitched giggle.

Hen makes the same face she did when she'd taken a huge swallow the morning the milk was off and everyone suspected it was Juanita Fernandez who'd unplugged the kitchen refrigerators.

'Don't be mean to her.'

'I'm just telling her the facts of life. It's better to know. Look what happened to Tina Bell! She had to find out from Gertie!'

The bell rings for break and we troop along the

corridor, down the stairs and into the freezing quad where the wind blows up our skirts and round our legs as we stamp up and down, waiting for the Saturday treat, sugared doughnuts.

We stand huddled around the tea urn.

'Hey, is it true, we have to move back to Yellow D after sheets?'

'What day is sheets?'

'Monday.'

'Do we?'

'Who said?'

'Gobby told our room on Friday.'

I walk over to the low wall with my tea. I thought we were staying at Merton the whole term. I look down the road by the netball courts, past the games teacher's house and into the trees.

I don't want to leave Merton.

There you can look at the red leaves and the flickering shadows and the sun glowing through them. You can hear the owls hoot at night from the wood that leads to the river. They call in breathing, shivering voices and sometimes clear like flutes, and the sound echoes off the marsh. You can look at the violet sky in the morning before the frosty walk to Mass, and the tree that grows out of the circle of earth, and dream of the path to the listening place. And in the evening I can walk away from the classrooms and the cold chapel and the stories that float like ribbons in the air.

But then my heart sinks further. Because it's more than leaving Merton. It's going back. Back to the dorm. Back to the De Profundis after lights out, the patrolling nun and the glimmering orange light. Back to the dark shape in the ceiling that descends at night and presses on your chest. The ghost girl that whispers something terrible into the lonely blackness, the one who cries in the pit of the night, cries into your ear and breathes into words the one terror you don't want to hear: 'Maybe you've done something wrong, maybe you've done something wrong, and that's why you've been sent away.' It cries in the night and I don't hear it at Merton. But in the dorm, the long corridor of curtains and the high ceiling, I know it's there crying, and every night it shivers in the hollow dark and makes me pull the covers over my head and curl up.

Miss Bolt comes out of her dark-green house and walks off down the road. She is free to come and go as she pleases.

I have to turn away from her freedom in case I panic, and start breathing quickly like I did in the restaurant toilet when I couldn't open the lock. They had to get the manager to come and talk to me through the keyhole so I calmed down.

'Can I borrow them to draw my own picture?'

'Yes, but don't use the gold or silver.'

'I don't want to use the gold or silver.'

I want to draw a picture of Very and me in the hammock under the stars.

'Don't use that red, though, use that one.'

'Can I use the blue?'

'No. Pick out the ones you want to use and I'll tell you if you can or not.'

Very stole it out of the chest at the bottom of the stairs. The one with the flowers painted on it that is under the mirror in London now. It was a huge string hammock, woven with different-coloured threads, that coiled about itself like a rainbow snake.

'Yes, yes, no, and yes.'

'Just those three?'

'Well, OK, you can use those two as well.'

It was the day after the fiesta and we'd stayed up half the night to watch the smiling and clapping and colourful dancing through the bars of the town-hall courtyard. The band played music that hooted and tooted and clashed and strummed in a sliding rhythm that made you want to jig about.

It was still playing the same jolly rhythms in the back pews the next morning, so the church was filled with the colossal sound and Padre Pedro had to frown all through the sermon to make up for the spoilt solemnity.

We climbed out the window with the hammock and walked along the yellow road in the heat where the day before we'd followed the procession of women with flowers on their heads, and gigantic swaying puppets dressed in bright clothes, steered inside by sweating men, the little children running after them shouting, the very little ones holding their mothers' hands with their

mouths wide open in astonishment, and coloured con-
fetti in their hair.

The road was scattered with wilting flower heads, and
strings of blue-and-white tissue-paper decorations fluttered in the breeze, some broken and dragging in the
yellow mud.

We walked past the crying tree into the singing forest
where bright-red birds flitted with black wings and blue-
green dragonflies like threads of coloured light darted in
the beams. Then the sunlight turned pink and set
quickly behind hills.

The warm night had a musical sound and smelt of
herbs.

Very tied the knots. She chose the trees and slung the
rope over and hoisted the hammock up while I held the
ends. The first try didn't work. I had to sit in it, to test it,
and I came thudding to the ground. Very had to test it
next time and bounce up and down really hard to prove
to me it wouldn't fall.

A wasp stung Very on the eyelid and her eye swelled
up, though she put a dry stick behind her ear. Then the
night was alive and full of sound. Shrieking metal
instruments and softly clacking sticks, and luminous
flashing lights which lit up the leaves or stalks of grass.

We watched the moon and the stars, and turned over
to warm the chilly part of our backs against each other,
so the hammock creaked and swung, and Very told me
stories of the people who lived in the cloud forests and
talked to trees and could make themselves invisible.
They were probably there right now, watching over us.

But the night grew cold and we woke before the sun, shivering, and had to get out of the hammock and jump around to get warm. We walked back along the path, frozen stiff, and down the hill and along the yellow road and back in the window just as the sun was beginning to rise up from behind the hill we'd just walked down.

'You've got the moon the wrong way round.'

'No, I haven't.'

'And stars aren't like that. Stars are like this, I'll show you.'

'Don't listen to her. I think it's a really good drawing.'

'It's good, I didn't say it wasn't good. It's just stars don't look like that and the moon's the wrong way round, and anyway what are they doing trapped in a net?'

'It's a HAMMOCK!'

There is a smell of bonfires when we walk up the school drive in our brown cloaks and out the school gates and along the sodden track in single file with two nuns with clipboards, one at the front and one behind. We pass houses behind hedges and gardens you can see through the bare twigs where children who are free are playing on a swing. We have to go on the school walk. Unless you are one of Sister Campion's chosen few who do wooding in the Merton woods, and make bonfires and are allowed to wear home clothes. They roast marsh-mallows in the flames and the rest of us are envious and pretend we don't care. We see them going up the track in a little gang with Sister Campion, her veil tied in a knot and her skirt hitched up, striding among them in her walking boots. Sister Campion is such 'good fun' – everyone says so.

We come to the end of the path and join a wide stony track and the single file rearranges itself into linked best friends. We go through the brown creaking gate like an army being ticked off on the clipboard. You have to report and be ticked off at the beginning then report and be ticked off at the end.

The walk is along the paths between rows and rows of Forestry Commission fir trees planted so close together that you can't walk amongst them. The tracks are long and straight and cross each other at right angles. It would be easy to lose yourself in this grid of identical pathways. The ash-coloured earth is printed with tyre tracks and footsteps.

Now and then we see a magpie, or a rabbit with myxomatosis, its eyes swelled up and blind, moving slowly to get under the tufty patches of heather to hide from danger it can't see.

I find myself walking along beside Eliza and Pen. 'Fake Scotland', Eliza calls this place. 'No one in their right mind would *choose* to walk here,' she says.

Pen and Eliza are best friends, but they look like opposites. Eliza has straight black hair, a fringe, and a pale face. She looks at you sideways with half-closed eyes.

Pen's eyes are wide open, and blue – they dart towards Eliza to see if she's said the right thing. She is short with tight yellow curls and freckles all over her face, on her hands, up her arms. She is touchy about her hair being called red. It's blonde. Strawberry-blonde is all right, but not red. Only Frizzy's hair is red.

Pen's blue eyes dart towards Eliza, then with a sly look at me she says, 'We think you've got a crush on Tony.'

'See if she blushes, see if she blushes,' Eliza joins in.

I feel myself reddening.

Tony is the head girl. She supervises the refectory queue, with one brown leg hitched up against the radiator so the muscles bulge out and all seven swimming badges sewn on to her gym shorts. She has a flick-back haircut.

'I have not!'

'Have so! Have so! Cath's got a crush!'

'We can tell, we can see it. Maybe we should tell Tony.'

'Shall we write her a little love note from you?'

I look into the dead fir trees. If I don't answer maybe they'll stop.

I had a fllick-back haircut once, after Very took me to the hairdresser. I told her to pick me up outside, not to come in. I was ashamed of my hair when I went to the hairdresser. I was even more ashamed of Very's. They cut my hair and flicked it back. I thought it was perfect.

The hairdresser said. 'It looks like real hair now.'

But Very was appalled.

'Real?' It looks like plastic! It's awful!'

Anyway it didn't last long. In the morning it was growing its own way again.

We walk along in silence for a while.

'So, you've joined the farmyard now, have you?' says Eliza, looking out the corner of her half-shut eyes. She clucks softly.

'What are you, the cow?' Pen giggles and her blue eyes dart from my face to Eliza's. She puts her fist over her mouth and says, 'Moo!' from behind her hand and giggles again, and looks at Eliza.

'She hasn't got a best friend,' says Eliza to Pen, 'so she's in the farmyard.'

'In the pigsty,' giggles Pen from behind her hand, and snorts.

'Poor little new girl, doesn't have a best friend,' Eliza says in a soft sing-song.

'I do so have one!'

'Oh yeah? Who?'

'Olive.'

'Four-eyes Olive?'

'Since when?'

'How should I know?'

'Says who?'

'Ask her!'

'Why aren't you walking with her then?'

'What? D'you think we're joined at the hip?' I heard a Lower Five say this in the supper queue. I don't know what it means, but nor does Eliza.

'Bet you she isn't.'

'She is.'

'What d'you bet then?'

'Don't know.'

'Bet you two holy cards.'

'OK, but not till after holy shop.'

'Not till after holy shop,' mimics Pen and smirks at Eliza.

But Eliza is looking ahead to see if she can spot Olive.

Tuck shop is Wednesday, but holy shop is after our walk. It sells white plastic rosary beads, missals, black-nylon lace mantillas, and hundreds of gilt-edged holy cards. The girls pore over the haloed lambs, and large-eyed infants with wings, and while they are bent over Pen and Eliza run their hands up and down girls' backs looking for a bra strap and, if they find one, ping it and then the word goes round, Tina Bell is wearing a BRA! And before long the whole class knows and Tina goes red whenever she catches anyone's eye.

'Where's Olive?' she asks Frizzy.

'Back that way,' says Frizzy.

'Come on. I'm going to ask her!'

I feel embarrassed.

'Oh don't ask her now!'

I knew Olive was on the walk – it's just sometimes you have to leave her on her own.

'Scared she'll say no?'

'That proves it, she's lying.'

'You owe me two holy cards,' says Eliza.

'No, I do not.'

'Right then, let's ask her.'

I sigh and follow them back through the walkers. Olive is ambling along, looking at the ground.

'Hey, Olive Oyl,' says Pen.

Olive looks up. Eliza and Pen are ants on the surface of the earth. She raises her eyebrows.

'Is Cath your best friend or not?'

Olive looks from Eliza to me with her puzzled magnified eyes.

'Yes,' she says.

Eliza presses her lips together and says nothing. She stomps off with Pen trotting behind.

I walk beside Olive. I feel awkward.

'Sorry, Olive.'

'What d'you mean, sorry? It's what we agreed.'

The cohort turns left and we walk down a track between slender silver birch trees with black splits like wide-open eyes on their white trunks, and the crumbly black earth is printed with hoof-marks filled with rain-water.

Olive tells me there is a blink in matter, it only looks solid. Really it's there, and then it's not there, and we spend the rest of the walk opening and closing our eyes very fast to see if we can catch the moment when nothing exists.

Sunday letter-writing is like study. We sit in the class-room and Sister Campion invigilates at the tall desk. She is reading her prayer book to herself. It makes a thick silence round her.

Everyone is bent over their desks. Only the clock ticking and the scratchy sliding sounds of calligraphy pens disturb the dense quietness.

You have to leave the opened envelope on Sister Campion's desk when you're finished. Very thinks these formal, carefully written letters are funny, because they are so stilted. But I wish I had invisible ink to write between the lines like they do in prison camps.

Dear Very,

Olive says we have twenty-five billion miles of DNA in our body, enough to reach to the moon and back five million times.

She says she wants to be an astrophysicist.

I still don't know. Maybe a zoologist. Then I could slide about on ropes with the monkeys in the Amazon rainforest and you could visit me in my hut, and it would all be dripping and steaming, and really muddy. Or we could go to the Arctic, with all that space, and look at the penguins.

Olive says sun spots send electrified particles to the magnetic poles and that's why you get the aurora borealis. It swirls like a rainbow curtain. We could see that too.

She says when she's become an astronaut (I said I thought you said astrophysicist, but that's only the first step) and she's in the rocket capsule, she'll turn all the lights out in the space craft and look at the stars.

The weather here is dismal, I hope London is nicer.

I am doing the history project with Piggy and Hen.

If you ask me, Olive doesn't need a space ship to see the stars. In fact I don't think Olive arrived when she was born. On the way in she got distracted and decided to stay up there, looking at red dwarfs and blue suns and star nurseries and supernovas, and the sixty-mile-high geysers on Triton.

I'm glad she's here, though, even if most of her isn't.

Write soon, love Catherine.

PS. *Savage Messiah* got confiscated.

When letter-writing is over we are allowed quiet re-creation and Sister Campion stops reading her missal. Piggy and Hen play cat's cradle, passing ever more elaborate string constructions between them. Mouse and Tessa do the crossword and call out clues.

Natalie pulls out her magazine to look at the fashion pictures with a mischievous look at Sister Campion. We aren't allowed magazines except in Saturday rec. Natalie slides her finger down the picture of a gold jumpsuit, and says, 'Isn't it gorgeous, Sister,' and I wonder what it's like, to bask in the warmth of Sister Campion's high regard.

Natalie has stacks of magazines in her common-room locker, she even has *Elle* in French, and shaves her legs with Ladyshave. She is on a diet to keep slim, and knows all about what to eat for hair, teeth and nails. Tessa uses Clearasil on the spots along her hair-line, but Natalie says it's sugar. Mouse says the pores are clogged with dirt and she can say it because she's been Tessa's best friend since Junior School.

They don't get spots in Junior School or use deo-dorant, Alpine Fresh and Sea Breeze. Juniors don't have to shave their arm pits or go on diets.

They're not spotty, fat and hairy, that's why.

I hate being thirteen.

I have an empty feeling when I walk up the road to Merton, after letter-writing. We have to pack up our things before benediction.

I walk into the room at Merton after tea. Pen and Eliza have already packed and are lying on a bed, reading magazines. The late afternoon sun shines through the red creepers. I open my drawers and lay my shirts on the bed.

'Don't you even notice us?'

'Here we are sitting watching you and you don't even say hello,' says Pen.

'Sorry,' I say, turning. 'I'm just getting my things ready.'

'Come and sit down on the bed.' Pen suddenly changes. 'Come and read magazines with us.'

'Yes, come and give us your opinion.'

I walk across and sit on the bed.

'Look what we've been looking at. We're deciding what to wear for the wedding, it's in a marquee, we need a long dress. Have you ever worn a long dress?'

'No,' I say. 'My sister has.'

They titter and look at each other.

'Look at this one.' She points to a lilac-striped gown with frills.

I shake my head.

'No, you're right. It is a bit old-fashioned.'

'I want a black dress anyway,' says Eliza, and stretches out on the bed. 'To go with my black hair.'

She nudges Pen. 'Get on with it', says the nudge, and hangs in the air between us. Get on with what?

'We've decided to ask for a five-room next term. We think it would be fun.'

'Better than the dorm,' I agree.

'D'you want to be in a five-room with us?'

I nod.

'OK.'

'But it's just . . . well, we're wondering about Piggy.'

Piggy comes from a farm. There are acres of fields behind her eyes and straw bales. I like Piggy. She stands up for people.

'We're . . . you know.'

'What?'

'Well, we were thinking of asking Laura to share with us instead of Piggy.'

'What do you think?'

'I don't mind,' I say.

'Don't you like Laura?'

'Wouldn't you prefer Laura?'

'I mean look, Piggy . . .'

'What *do* you think of her anyway?'

'She's a bit boring, isn't she?'

I look from one to the other, both eager, looking at my face. I look at the trees, the sunlight is on the floor, a late sun, deep-yellow light. I want to be friends with them. I swallow.

'Piggy's all right,' I say.

'What about that haircut!' says Eliza, looking at me from my head all the way down to my shoes, examining my shoes as if she smells a bad smell, then back to my face.

'Yeah, it's not that great,' I say, picking up the straggly ends of my hair.

'No, Piggy, stupid! Piggy's haircut!'

'Oh,' I say.

'Have you ever seen her in her home clothes?'

'No,' I shake my head.

'She's a swot anyway, isn't she.'

'Yeah,' I say. I long to join in with them, give them what they want, but I can't think of anything to say.

'So you obviously don't mind sharing with her.'

I shrug.

'No ... I suppose. I mean it doesn't make any difference. I'll share with Laura.'

They look at one another.

'All right, Piggy, you can come out!'

Piggy comes out from under the bed looking sheepish. This is not her idea. We catch each other's eye, we are both ashamed.

'We're testing everyone to see if we can trust them,' says Pen.

Eliza holds her hand up.

'Shsh! Frizzy's coming.'

'Get back under!' orders Pen.

Piggy slips reluctantly under the bed. They look at me.

'Sit down on the bed.'

I feel horrified.

'Oh get on with your packing. There isn't enough room for you anyway.'

I go and sit down on my bed. The sun has gone and I look out into the twilit evening. The creeping leaves have become dark shapes. I fold up my home clothes and put them in my canvas bag.

Frizzy is a fat girl with fuzzy hair that grows in all directions. 'Pubes on her head,' said Eliza. Her face is big, with a bulbous forehead, and thick eyebrows.

Frizzy opens the door.

'Hi Frizzy!' says Eliza.

'Hi,' says Frizzy, standing in the doorway.

'Well, aren't you going to come in?' says Pen from the bed.

Frizzy stands in the doorway lit from behind. Her cardigan is buttoned to the wrong buttons. She has dainty feet.

'Come and sit on the bed with us – we're looking at magazines.'

Frizzy is flattered.

'Oh are you?' she says.

'Look at this tartan jumpsuit,' says Eliza.

'Oh it's lovely!' says Frizzy, sitting on the edge of the bed.

'Isn't it gorgeous!'

'Do you like him?' says Eliza, folding out the middle-page spread of Barry Manilow.

Frizzy nods.

'Did you have a good half term?' says Pen.

Frizzy nods.

'What did you do?'

'I was at home and we . . .'

'Any parties?'

Frizzy shakes her head.

'Well, never mind,' says Pen. 'Not everyone goes to parties.'

Frizzy looks from one to the other, trying to think of something to say, smiles and lifts her shoulders in a little jerk.

'Come on, Frizzy, get right up on the bed and get comfy.'

She pulls her dainty feet on to the eiderdown.

'Did you make any new friends?'

She shakes her head.

'Well, never mind. We're your friends, aren't we.'

'You don't need any new ones.'

Her white skin blushes with pleasure.

'It's so nice sharing a room with friends, don't you think, Frizzy?'

'Oh yes!' she says, 'I'm thrilled.'

'Shame we're moving back to the dorm.'

'Yes,' says Frizzy, 'it's such a shame.'

'We want to ask for a five-room next term.'

'D'you want to share with us?'

Frizzy nods vigorously, her hair quivering.

'Trouble is . . .' says Eliza, and looks at Pen.

'Yes, trouble is . . .' says Pen, and looks at Frizzy.

'What?' says Frizzy.

'Piggy Ham,' says Eliza.

'What?' says Frizzy.

'Well, I mean . . . Piggy Ham.'

Frizzy looks from one to the other.

'She doesn't exactly FIT with us, does she?'

'Know what I mean?'

Frizzy nods.

'We thought maybe we could ask Laura to share instead of Piggy.'

Frizzy nods again.

'What do you think of Piggy?'

Frizzy looks unsure.

'Well, she's a bit . . . you know.'

'What?' say Eliza and Pen together.

She squirms and looks at the ceiling.

'Boring?' mouths Pen.

'Boring!' says Frizzy, glad to be helped out.

'Anything else?'

'Well, she's not very pretty,' says poor Frizzy.

'No, she's not very pretty . . . and?'

'And she doesn't fit,' says Frizzy.

Pen looks at her with a flat-eyed look and says, 'Piggy, you can come out now!'

A look of horror passes across Frizzy's face. She swallows and turns red to the roots of her frizzy red hair, and, as Piggy emerges from under the bed, Frizzy's face wrinkles up, she bursts into tears and runs out of the room. Piggy looks sad.

'Now you know who your friends are!' says Pen.

Eliza nods with her lips pressed together and her eyebrows raised.

Piggy walks across to her bed, puts on the side-light and opens her case, then with a great deal of concentration she begins to fold up her clothes. Piggy and Frizzy have always been allies. Not friends, but allies.

She only does it because she's mad on Mr Perkins.'

'Rubbish, it's the outfit.'

'Mr Perkins, don't you like my tight white breeches?' says Mouse.

'It's because she's French. They do it for posture.'

'Is she going to be all right, though?' says Hen.

'Course.'

'No thanks to Ethelbug.'

'What happened? Did someone phone her mother?'

'The Upper Six on my table said she was green. Ethelbug gave her Milk of Magnesia and told her to go back to class!'

'Typical.'

'What was it then?'

'Twisted gut! She could have died.'

'Poor Natalie!'

'They took her to hospital in an ambulance.'

'Doesn't exactly inspire confidence.'

'Who's ever had confidence in Ethelbug? She's got senile dementia.'

'She gives out Valium like aspirin.'

'Fenella's collected ten.'

'What for? She going to top herself next?'

'No, her brother told her if you dissolve them in Coca-Cola you get high.'

'Chop chop, girls,' says Miss Bolt, putting her head round the corner of the alcove. 'I'd like the benches brought out on to the floor, this side of tomorrow, please and thank you.'

Before half term Fenella had run away. The nuns had found her on the road at night, on the way to the station, with make-up on. They were very worried about the make-up.

We lift up a heavy shiny bench and carry it out into the gym. You have to walk up and down the squeaking wood and jump around at the end, all in one go. I can never see the point of the benches. Why on earth do that?

But it's true about Sister Ethelburga. I'd woken her myself in the second week of term, because I couldn't sleep. I'd knocked on her door and when she opened it she was wearing a long white nightgown and a white cloth helmet, tied in a bow under her chin. She looked like a baby in a christening dress.

'How DARE you waken me at night. How DARE you!'

She was livid. Her cheeks went pink, and her jowls wobbled. A wrinkled angry baby.

I was glad to get back to my bed. If I'd been scared by anything, it was nothing compared to that.

The next day she gave me five Valium in an envelope, and I passed them on to Fenella because I'd heard she collected them.

After we've walked up and down the benches we pull the horse out, and the springboard, and the green spongy mats that lie in a pile in the alcove next to the fencing equipment.

'Spot on!' says Miss Bolt as the games captain flies over the horse doing the splits and lands with her feet together.

My hands and legs become mysteriously tangled on the horse and I have to climb over it.

'Mats, please, girls!'

The gym is large and light with a bouncy wooden floor with springs in it, painted with red-and-white stripes for indoor netball.

We lie on the spongy mats.

Mr Perkins is the fencing master. I have seen Natalie and the games captain dressed in white doing 'on guard' with him through the little window in the gym door.

'Shoulder stand, please!'

I am thinking about Mr Perkins in his white breeches when Miss Bolt kneels down next to my mat and mouths something. I look at her pearly lips and nod because she is nodding.

'You just lie still, dear,' she says, and gets up to order everyone into handstands.

In the cold locker room we change out of gym clothes.

'Have you got it then?' says Piggy, unbuttoning her Aertex shirt.

'What?'

'The curse,' she whispers.

'No.'

'What did you tell Miss Bolt?'

'I didn't tell her anything.'

'Well, why didn't you do the shoulder stand? You're not supposed to do that if you've got the curse.'

'I don't know. She came and mouthed something at me. I just nodded.'

Piggy snorts.

'You'll have to pretend you've got it every month – she keeps a little book.'

'I've got a sore tummy, Pigs. D'you think I'm getting it?' says Hen.

'Go and see Sister Ethelburga,' says Eliza. 'She'll probably take your appendix out.'

The bell rings and we walk along the corridors in a crowd to collect our knitting from the needlework lockers.

The needlework room has windows that reach the floor. They look over the tennis courts and into the woods and the path that leads to Merton. We are knitting cardigans for the mission schools this term. There are photographs on the board of small African children in last year's lopsided cardigans. Their faces glow and shine in the hot sunlight. I wonder if they really need cardigans in Africa.

'Natalie should sue.'

'Don't be stupid – nuns don't have any money!'

'They do so! Sister Campion was an heiress! She brought a huge dowry to the convent.'

'Do nuns have dowries?' Hen says.

The others look up in case Sister Anne is listening.

'Do they?'

Sister Anne's tall willowy body is stooped over the yellow wooden table. Her chair is too low. We queue up with our grimy knitting so she can untangle it, redo it, or pick up the stitches we have dropped.

'Lucy, why are your needles always sticky?'

'Sorry, Sister.'

'Don't you wash your hands?'

'Yes, Sister.'

Sister Anne speaks on a minor note. She has smooth white translucent skin like the wax doll in the V & A with its cool beautiful glass eyes. She shakes her head at my knitting and takes it off the needles and undoes several rows, so the wool is crinkled.

I look down at her profile, her eyelashes and her long neck. There is a sadness around Sister Anne. I walked into it once, it was by the window, a longing so intense it made me gasp and hold my breath. Maybe she felt it when she looked out over the trees.

'Concentrate, dear, you keep dropping stitches,' she says, and looks at me with blue faraway eyes.

I take my undone knitting back to my place to start again.

'OK, I'll swap you two cheeses for an apple.'

'No, I told you, I want the cheese with my apple.'

'Why? It's just about time for fish and chips,' says Lucy.

'FAST day!' they say together.

On fast day we have soup and rolls and offer up our hunger for the African missions. Today the thin smell of onion soup is salting the air.

'Poor Natalie won't be getting much – can you eat with a twisted gut?'

'What do they do? Open you up and untwist it?'

'Who knows.'

'Well, it'll be good for her diet.'

'The flesh is the greatest of all our enemies,' says Lucy in a wobbly voice like Father Finnigan's.

'That girl's a beanpole.'

'We must fight it all the days of our life!'

'Oh shut up, Lucy.'

'My sister says she'll get anorexia.'

'Anorexia?'

'When you don't eat.'

'Sister Anne's probably got it,' whispers Lucy.

'Skinny malinky long legs!'

'With umbrella feet,' says Eliza.

'Went to the cinema and couldn't find a seat,' they all join in.

'When the film show started –'

'Skinny malinky farted –'

And everyone bursts out laughing.

'More work and less noise,' says Sister Anne in her high voice, without looking up.

The chapel smells of incense from yesterday's Mass.

Mother Perpetua is taking upstairs choir practice with the Upper School. The gold on the altar is flickering in the light of the candle in a red jar.

Mouse comes out of the door that leads to the

confessional and genuflects in the side aisle, then slips into the pew behind and kneels down with a sigh. I wonder if she has been given a big penance. The girl next to me gets up and goes into the confessional box, and I slip along the pew. I am next – it's like waiting for the dentist.

Mother Perpetua taps the lectern with her conducting stick and they all breathe in and sing. The high slow notes rise up to the ceiling and intertwine.

I am kneeling beside Sister Anne. She must be fighting the flesh. Her long slender body is folded over and she is holding her rosary so tight there must be an indent in her fingers. I watch her eyeballs move back and forth under the lids. She is hardly breathing.

The door creaks open and it's my turn to go through, and sit down next to the black grille.

I am nervous. I can hear breathing.

'Bless me, Father, for I have sinned. It is three weeks since my last confession.'

I am kneeling in the musty dark little box. I can see the shape of the priest's head behind the grille, bent over, listening.

'Yes, my child,' he says in a low voice.

I breathe in, wait, trying to get the courage.

'I think it's gluttony, Father,' I say quickly as I breathe out.

'Yes, my child, go on.'

I thought I could get away with just saying what the sin was, but that isn't enough.

'Fish fingers,' I say.

'Yes, my child?'

He wants the whole story.

'Well, Natalie didn't want her fish fingers, Father. Because of her diet she says fried food . . . well, so I had them, but then when Jenny sat down, well, she doesn't like . . . well, I had hers too, and I had one of the Lower Five's as well, well, two.'

'And how many fish fingers does that make altogether?'

'Fourteen.'

I hear a sniff behind the grille. I think he is shocked. And he says the words of absolution in a low voice and gives me penance.

I cross myself and leave with relief and kneel down again next to Sister Anne to do my penance, which is two rosaries. That makes it seven Hail Marys, an Our Father, and a Glory Be per fish finger which I think is a bit steep, as four of the fish fingers were mine to begin with.

Two rosaries take a long time. I'm worried about getting a good place in the telephone queue, and Sister Anne is still fighting. I'm sure she is because her knuckles are white, and she keeps holding her breath and letting it go in a quick sigh. The air is disturbed with her painful feelings and I want to pull on her arm and say, 'Stop that, please stop doing that'.

Finally I finish and slide along the pew and walk quickly down the side aisle, past the statue of Jesus with his heart showing outside his clothes, past the holy water, and I remember I have forgotten to genuflect and, when I turn round to dip my fingers in the water, I see it under the carved stone bowl, a tiny transparent being made of light, and I know it must be Sister Anne's, scared out of her by the sound of her grinding mind.

And I can't bear to look at it, so I run through the double doors of the chapel and through the swing doors into the corridor outside the refectory with its smell of boiled cabbage, boiled years ago, still lingering in the air.

After the phone call with Very the world inside me is full of Soho, the purple sky and the twinkling lights of the city night, the flavours of Very's freedom, and so different from the stone floor and the corridor to the classrooms, that I have to sit down on a bench no one sits on because it's on the way somewhere, and close my eyes. I hold on to the seat.

'Are you all right, dear?'

I am startled by a large-faced nun leaning over me.

'Oh yes, fine, Sister, thank you.'

'Was it a telephone call?'

I cannot possibly tell her what Very has just told me. I nod.

'What was it, dear?'

I want her to leave me alone with Very's voice.

She sits down and takes my hand on her lap. She pats it reassuringly.

'You can tell me, dear.'

Her face shows concern, but her eyes gleam with nosiness.

It's hard to make up a story when you haven't digested the true one. Anyway, Very's all right, that's the main thing, though she was depressed about the job in the bookie's – they sacked her the same day.

'Why, Very?'

'I panicked.'

'Why?'

'I got screamed at.'

'Why?'

'Couldn't do it, couldn't add up all those numbers, couldn't work the till.' And then she sighed. 'What's wrong with me? I can't do normal things.'

I said it was fine to do abnormal things.

But it was because of what happened. She was depending on that money, she said. Now she'd never see a penny and the painting was just about finished.

'Just tell me all about it, dear!' The nun squeezes my trapped hand.

Very said she and Big Terry's friend Cragg stood outside for ages in the cold, smoking roll-up cigarettes on the corner next to the Chinese supermarket, so they could watch the door of the club.

Very said Cragg kept saying, 'It ain't the first time,' as if it would all be fine.

'A family friend, Sister.'

'Yes?' she says with eagerness. 'Tell me, dear, you'll feel much better.'

The lucky thing was they didn't put Very in the car. They'd all arrived at once, no knocking, Cragg was there to open the door but they kicked it down.

'Stupid thugs,' Big Terry said. 'Watching too much telly, that's what that's from.'

They had Big Terry with his hands on the wall.

'Could you mind your manners?' he said.

'A family friend?'

'Yes, Sister.'

They said, 'Who's this floozy?' pointing at Very.

Big Terry said, 'Please!'

Very said, 'I'm painting his interior.'

The policewoman said, 'Come with us, luv,' and held her by the elbow.

That's when her charcoal fell on the floor and all the men started crunching it into the orange carpet, and Big Terry started shouting that they had no respect for property. That's when the superintendent told Very she could go.

So she waited outside with Cragg in the cold, until they saw Big Terry being led out in handcuffs. The policewoman put her hand on his head when he got in the car, as though he was a little boy, Very said, to stop him banging his head.

Cragg was almost crying. But Very was worrying about the sixty-five pounds for the painting that was almost finished.

'Is the family friend in difficulties, dear?'

'He's lost his business, Sister.'

'Oh I'm sorry to hear that, dear. It's hard when a friend falls on hard times.'

'Yes, Sister.'

* * *

Up four flights of shining wooden stairs that smell of polish are the unpolished wooden steps that lead to the piano rooms. I walk along the narrow corridor listening to the dissonant layers of plinking melodies, chords and scales.

The room with the slanted ceiling is just big enough for a piano, and looks over the trees, and far beyond the school boundaries, to a curved river reflecting the sky, snaking its way east into the setting darkness.

I never practise. I never even open the book. I just sit here staring, listening to the sounds, looking out the window, knowing that, for half an hour, no one will open the door.

Sister Gertrude sits at the end of Yellow D with her head bowed, holding her rosary and turning it slowly, the silver crucifix with a miniature Jesus nailed to it dangling down. She turns each of the pale-blue crystal beads back and forth between her thumb and her forefinger, and her lips move silently. There is something spooky about seeing her lips move without even a whisper coming out, and they move very fast.

It was Sister Gertrude Tina Bell had to go to the morning she got her period, the first one in our class. Tina had to say, 'Im bleeding, Sister,' because she didn't know what was happening. But Sister Gertrude didn't tell her any biology or the facts of life, she just went to the cupboard and brought out an enormous sanitary pad and a belt with metal hooks and gave it to Tina Bell to wear.

'Here,' she said, 'you're lucky! I've been bleeding for twenty years.'

I walk by with my towel over my arm, and my washbag. You mustn't put your towel over your shoulder because its unladylike.

'Where d'you think you're going, into a boxing ring?' Sister Gertrude had said, and I'd thought of the newspaper photograph of Dave Boy Green sellotaped to the fridge that Very had pointed at, nodding, with her mouth full of bacon sandwich, when I'd asked her if she believed in God.

I walk along the brown corridor and up the stairs to the bathrooms. I'm not going to have a bath, it's not my bath night. We get two a week and, if you're found having a bath when it's not your night, it's five conduct marks and straight to Mother Agatha.

I take out my toothbrush, and look in the mirror. Sometimes I don't know who it is looking back. I say, 'Who are you?' to my reflection, but the face looks bewildered.

Someone bangs on the door.

'I haven't been in here long!' I say, taking the toothbrush out of my mouth.

'I don't care – it's my bath night and I want a long one. Get out of there, Lower Four.'

It's Amelia Stowe from the Upper School – you don't argue with her. I hurriedly wipe my face, and stupidly apologise as I open the door. I hate that, I hate that I apologise when it's not my fault. I walk back along the dark corridor.

The nuns don't get many baths either. That's why they have their smells. Sister Scholastica smells of metal. Sister Gobnet smells of something milky that has gone sour and Mother Agatha smells of burnt things.

Sister Gertrude smells of fish glue. I pass her and she hasn't moved. Her lips are still travelling fast as she races through the beads. She has a devotion to the sacred heart, and last week was her Feast Day. The shelf above her head is covered with Feast Day cards of the Sacred Heart. We have been doing circulation with Miss Tweedie, and 'the hollow muscular organ whose con-traction propels blood through the circulatory system'. Some of the pictures are blood-red and shining, com-plete with ventricles and aorta.

She finishes her rosary and she sits with two vertical lines above her nose, as though she has her eyes crossed under the lids. Her hands are folded, holding the rosary. The blue beads match her blue veins. Deoxygenated blood. Her face is white, a lurid white, with red eyebrows and a pinched look. Her shoes are tied up very tight.

She opens her eyes suddenly, like they do in horror films when you think they're dead. I jump. She smiles her see-through smile, with her jaw clenched and her eyes too wide, an insane person's smile. It is very uncomfortable being smiled at by Sister Gertrude. I slip through the yellow curtain into my dim cubicle.

After lights out Sister Gertrude says in a high trem-bling voice, ' "Out of the depths I cry to thee, oh Lord," ' and we respond out of the blackness, '"Lord, hear my voice!"'

'"Let thine ears be attentive to the voice of my supplication."'

But I don't think God listens.

'Is that all she said? "I've been bleeding for twenty years,"' everyone was anxious to know.

'Yes, that's all,' said Tina, 'but then she smiled.'

And everyone felt sorry for Tina because Sister Gertrude had smiled and told her a strange secret, and secrets about Sister Gertrude are not altogether safe. It's better to get them second-hand.

We all know the story of Katie Smith, in Yellow D after lights out, when Sister Gertrude had opened the curtain of her cubicle and sat down on the bed. Katie Smith thought it was a black ghost, her heart was beating so fast she couldn't move or speak, and Sister Gertrude had picked up her hand and scratched a soft scratch down her forearm and said, 'I'm a cat and this is how I show my affection.'

She'd slipped out of the cubicle into the blackness of the corridor and Katie Smith had been left stunned in the darkness, and the story made my hair stand on end because Katie is called Catherine and so was Sister Gertrude before she took the veil, and maybe that's what she meant by the cat. That makes me a cat too, doesn't it? And maybe she'll come through *my* curtain one night after the De Profundis has made me scared, and pick up *my* forearm and tell me a chilling secret about bleeding her whole life.

I see a thin thread of blue light shining down the side of my cupboard. I kneel on my bed and stick my head under the bit of curtain on my side of the partition. The moon is shining on to the roof of the gym, on to the tarmac road and the trees. Olive has told me about the moon. The sea of clouds, the ocean of storms, the bay of rainbows, and the lake of the sleepers.

I get back into bed and hold the curtain up so there is a triangle of blue light on the cupboard. Olive says blue is a lazy colour. It travels from the sun in white light with the other colours, but it scatters before it reaches your eye. That's why the distance is always blue, and the sky. But I don't think that's laziness.

It's all because of Natalie's twisted gut, I think to myself as I pass her empty cubicle next door to mine. If it wasn't for that I wouldn't be closing the curtain in a hurry, undoing my tie, stepping out of my skirt, and pulling off my horrible knee-length beige socks. I rummage about in my blue canvas bag at the bottom of my cupboard, and shiver in my vest and pants.

I think it was last-minute, and pure luck. She just saw me walking down the corridor on the way to get my cloak, and she was standing next to the school-walk nun with the clipboard.

She said, 'We have a space on the wooding team. Would you like to join us?'

'Yes, Sister Campion,' I said straightaway. 'Yes, thank you.'

'Well, change quickly, dear, and catch us up. We'll be walking up the road towards Merton.'

As soon as I got round the corner, I belted up the stairs.

I pull on my jeans and my tartan shirt and my blue jersey. They all smell faintly of turpentine. Little fronds seem to unfurl in the air around me when I am standing there in my home clothes. I sit down on the edge of the yellow candlewick bedspread. I can breathe. I pull my hair out of its ponytail and put on my stripy hat pulled over my ears, and my Tottenham Hotspur football scarf that Eddie gave to Very.

I feel as if I am invisible as I walk through the school in my home clothes, an invisible visitor from another time. The rules of the convent don't touch me because I am in my home clothes.

I skip down the wooden stairs. The school is emptying out – even Upper Six and prefects have to walk those long avenues of identical muddy paths. I run down the corridor, past the classrooms and down the back stairs to the locker rooms. The walls are painted the colour of olives – green olives, which is not olive-green.

Girls are standing at their lockers, pulling on wellies.

'Hey, how come you're in home clothes?' says Eliza.

'I'm going wooding.'

'How come you're going wooding?'

I shrug.

'It's not fair – why should the new girl go?'

'Oh shut up about new girl. She's been here practically a whole term,' says Piggy.

'Still a bloody new girl.'

'Toast me a marshmallow,' says Piggy through her fringe.

I run out the arched door in my wellies and up the road towards Merton.

The favoured ones are in a gang around Sister Campion who is striding up the lane in her wellies with her habit hitched up into her skirt, carrying an oval wooden basket containing a small axe, a packet of firelighters and newspaper.

'Well done, dear,' she says. 'Natalie will be back next Saturday, but this week Catherine is joining us.'

Some of the gang look round and nod. There is Tessa who told on me, and her best friend Mouse, Jenny, and Tina Bell, who's got her period, and the games captain with her long dark plait.

We take the path through the rhododendrons into the wood.

'Who would like to clear the hearth?' She marks out the space with twigs. 'From here, to here.'

I volunteer, and the others move off in different directions to gather branches.

I lift clumps of newly fallen leaves from the patch to be cleared. They are orange and red with yellow veins. Underneath are the dry leaves, colourless and crackly like paper. Beneath them is the sodden dark mulch of decay. And underneath all the layers is the crumbly black earth, secretly growing the whole wood.

I clear a circle, and brush it with twigs, ready for the fire.

'We have a hearth!' says Sister Campion, returning with her arms full of branches, and letting them fall in a pile.

We roll the newspaper and plait it into kindling sticks.

Sister Campion builds a pyramid of twigs around the paraffin-smelling cakes hidden in the newspaper.

'More wood!' says Sister Campion.

When I return with my arms full, the fire is already crackling and leaping in high flames. I let my branches go in a cascade on to the heap. The fire has lit a wild flame in their eyes – I can see it flickering. There are squeals of hilarity. Even Sister Campion's face is flushed with heat and excitement.

'Feed the flames! Feed the flames!' chant Tessa and Mouse.

They run off in all directions to gather more sticks. I can hear them laughing and shouting, and cracking branches and twigs.

The fire burns into a glowing brilliance, and bright lilac flames flick back and forth in the fierce heat at the centre. I sit down next to the fire. I can hear the others in the trees behind me, sawing and chopping.

The fire has a life in it. I kneel down to look into the life of the fire and begin to talk. I tell it that I hate Sister Felicity, that I want to go home, and I miss Very. I tell it that I'm terrified of Mother Agatha, that I loathe geography, and I'm scared of Eliza. I whisper all my miseries, my hates and fears in a torrent of cracked words that I can't stop once they begin, and the fire gathers them all up and places them in its warm heart, spitting and licking with purple flames. I speak until I am emptied out then I look at the fire in silence.

'Watch out, this is going straight on the fire!' and a log with dry leaves is hurled on to the flames and each dry leaf still clinging to the twigs catches alight with a pale-orange flame. They put their offerings on to the fire, and we all sit down around the flames because that is enough for today.

Everyone looks expectantly at Sister Campion.

And she looks around with her eyebrows raised.

'Well, girls, I think we deserve a treat.'

'Yes!' they all cheer, and from the voluminous pocket she pulls out a big see-through packet of pink-and-white fluffy marshmallows. Those in the know have their long twiggy sticks at the ready to prong the prize.

Sister Campion ceremoniously opens the packet and sticks the marshmallows on the end of the outstretched sticks. I find a long twig in the leaves and stretch it towards her and she prongs a pink marshmallow on the end.

I poke my stick into the fire and watch the outside turn brown. I draw it back through the blue smoke. The toasted crust splits so the pink sticky sweet hot centre oozes through, melted and delicious. We eat our one marshmallow slowly and by the time we have finished the fire has burnt to glowing embers.

We cover the remains with earth and wet leaves and walk back through the woods as the sky streaks with glowing pink light and the sun goes down. Everyone has daubs of earth and charcoal on their faces and dirty hands, and I feel shot through with fire and the sweet taste of marshmallow and the sunset's streaks of light.

There is a scuffle in the classroom. Lucy has started a rolled-up-paper fight and is standing on a chair next to the bin aiming her missiles. Scrunched-up balls of paper are flying through the air.

'What's first lesson?'

'Sister Elastic. Calligraphy.'

I look at the green parrot.

'What's the point of smelling it?'

'I wanted to see if it smells of her perfume.'

The bird has a pink plume and a black-and-yellow eye, but the blue parrot is almost entirely obscured by the postmark.

'Well, aren't you going to open it?'

Hen has brought it from the letter bench. But I don't want to read it in here.

I walk out the classroom and along the corridor.

I wonder if they have porcupines in Indonesia.

I walk down the stairs towards the Middle School library. The toilets down here are dark and cold, and the air is filled with the poisonous disinfectant smell of the sanitary bins, but hardly anyone comes here. The date on the postmark is three weeks ago. It's like light years. Mummy is three weeks away.

I imagine the Foreign Office as a huge hand wearing a gold signet ring with a portcullis on it, that moves Daddy about the world like a chess piece. Very and I are attached on long strings like kites and we land in different places.

I remember the hot black sand and the fragrance of coconuts and spices, the warm air, and the shining eyes, and the little shop made of coconut palms, lit with a candle in the still, warm darkness. The pink sea at sunset, blue-green pale, and coconut milk through a straw and smooth orange papaya, the tumbling salt water and waves full of sand.

And I remember a city of white houses where we were locked inside a courtyard with men in black uniforms with white belts and silver buckles.

And then there were the dark hills that settled into a blue slumber. That is the home I remember most. With Conchita who smelt of chillies and chocolate, and the tree that cried resin tears from a machete cut that never healed.

I go into the toilet at the far end which has a little window and is lighter than the others. I lock the door and sit down on the toilet with the lid down.

I don't live anywhere now. I've never been to Jakarta. I got packed up along with the luggage and sent to school.

'But where will I go in the holidays, Mummy?'

'Oh you can stay with Verity, darling.'

'But I don't have a bedroom at Verity's, Mummy.'

'Oh darling, does it matter? You'll only be there a tiny bit. And you can come and visit us when it's all ready. Do stop wriggling.'

'I'm not wriggling.'

'Well, sit still then.'

I cried in the restaurant and held Very's hand under the table, and Mummy laughed her silvery laugh all through the film, to the accompaniment of her clinking bracelets when she raised her hands in the air.

I look at the round blue writing, spidering across the thin paper, round curly writing with flourishes. It reminds me of her curly blonde hair and how she sits in front of the mirror flicking her pearls and laughing at her own reflection.

When Mummy came to the flat, it became her flat and Very slept on the sofa in the sitting room. Mummy spread her pink-and-white cloth with lace edges on the chest of drawers and arranged her bottles and tubs of face cream and lotion, her lipsticks in rows, nail polish, mascara and powder. The flat smelt of her perfume, and she said, 'Darling do hide *those*!' to Very's box of Tampax.

'From who?' said Very, sighing and putting them in a cupboard.

'Whom,' corrected Mummy.

I open the envelope carefully so I don't tear the parrots. I don't know her really, but I yearn for her. It's like yearning for someone you've never met.

She lived another life while Very and I ran wild in the hot light, along the yellow road, under the blue trees that shed their petals on the ground. And she floated in and out of our lives in exquisitely tailored dresses like a cool perfumed world.

I unfold the paper.

Darling,

I hope you are settling in. We are doing our best here too. The house is in a dreadful disarray but we are coming along. Poor Daddy caught the most awful tummy bug. I've been arranging flowers this morning, meeting the ambassadors' wives and whatnot. It's rather fun in the market. We picked up all sorts of knick-knacks that I'm sure you'd adore. There's a rather charming restaurant near by that is convenient and fun. But what a drab dinner given for Daddy! I felt rather overdressed in my gold.

Do make sure Verity takes you to the hairdresser's next time you're out with her.

It's dreadfully muggy here, and for the last three days there's been no air-conditioning! Poor Daddy! It does take some time to get oneself used to a new city, and it is rather tiresome, but the maid has just brought in the most heavenly flowers so perhaps all will be well. There's really so much to organise! I can't find anything, and you know Daddy, he does fuss.

Write a long letter, darling. Remember to use both sides of the paper.

Love from Mummy.

I fold up the paper then unfold it and read it again.

Mummy was never cross. Not like Conchita who used to call on all the saints to witness our badness, our dirty hands or unfinished chicken.

But sometimes she had headaches, and she lay on the bed with her clothes on and a damp white flannel on her forehead and all the muscles by her eyes creased and tightened up if you walked by, or talked even in a whisper. They were awful, those headaches. I knew they were. I could see them scurrying across the ceiling like red spiders.

Mummy was only cross once that I can remember. When Very and I went to spy on the witch.

The bell rings for first lesson and I run up the stairs to be in the classroom in time for Sister Elastic.

PART THREE

P erhaps it was the blackberries. Or maybe it was the sunlight that made it happen. One of those soft, clear days with blue sky, when even going out to games is a pleasure, so you can walk along the path and feel the light and the shadows of bare branches cross over your eyelids. When you don't even mind standing in goal, if it's not the shadowed end, just so you can stand in the light. The yellow light. And the great blue space and the lit-up grass.

We were on upper pitch surrounded by trees. Only a few orange leaves left on the twigs, but heaps on the ground, swept to the edge of the pitch in maroon piles next to the stalky white grass and dead bracken. It was in the far corner that Lucy found them. After Miss Bolt had blown the whistle she strode away to lower pitch to call in the others. A harvest of blackberries, deep purple and shining. Growing in clusters among brilliant red leaves. A spider's web woven above them had caught a white feather, and a small dead leaf was spinning beneath it in midair from an invisible thread.

We gathered round and picked them off the tangled thorny branches, pricking our fingers, and scratching our arms, while Eliza chased Pen across the grass pressing blackberries down her back so her beige Aertex shirt had blobs of purple juice-stain.

Then someone said, 'Let's pick some for the others.'

You wouldn't think anyone would have cared, but something had happened, it was in the air, everyone wanted to join up, maybe it was the sun, but the blackberries helped, and we gathered more for the others and walked through the flickering sunlight with our games jerseys tied round like aprons, filled with fruit, singing, 'Walking on the beaches, looking at the peaches, NAH-nah nah', in a tribute to Fenella. In the hockey hut the others from middle and lower pitch were untying their bootlaces and rubbing the mud off their legs. They were amazed. And we spread the blackberries along the wooden benches for everyone to share.

'Wow, that's ridiculous!'

'At this time of year.'

'Thanks, you lot.'

The hut smelt of sweat.

'Who's ponging?'

Natalie, still a little pale, said she never told her mother there were no showers after games. The French are very hygienic.

Then we decided. We decided all together.

'Let's be late.'

'Who do we have?'

'Sister Felicity.'

'If we all have the same story . . .'

'We can say Miss Bolt's watch stopped.'

So we lounged around in the hockey hut until the blackberries were finished and wandered up to the locker room to change out of our Aertex shirts and games shorts into our pleated skirts and jerseys.

Sister Felicity was already in the classroom and her neck was flushed. I could tell by her face that she didn't believe us.

'Well, Lower Four, now that you've had your bit of fun, I think we can begin.'

She handed out the essays and I had 'Very good work' written in red. I don't think it was the lie we told that made her purse her lips as she handed out the exercise books. It was the threads that had been woven between us, like the spiders' webs between the brambles that twirl small leaves in thin air. She could sense it. And all through the lesson I watched her looking round at us, as though she was working out how strong it was, and how she could tear it apart.

And now I'm standing in the chapel queue for evening Mass, looking out the window at the twilight falling on the beautiful day, with the imprint of hands patting my back, because I thought the threads had broken and I was wrong.

We move in a double file, wearing our mantillas. Some are heirlooms of ancient lace, some are nylon from holy shop on Saturdays. I am holding my missal stuffed with holy cards. There is a quiet shuffle, and we can hear the faraway sounds of the organ playing the coming-in tune.

The file separates down both side aisles, and I sit in

the pew next to the prefect with the hooked nose. We stand up when the priest comes in, and the organ plays 'Soul of my saviour, sanctify my breast', and we sing, 'Deep in thy wounds, Lord, hide and shelter me,' and I imagine poor Jesus with his wounds that never heal, because we're all crowded in there like in a bus shelter, with blood dripping on us like rain.

'Stand up, please, Catherine,' Sister Felicity said at the end of the lesson, tapping the board pen in the flat of her hand, tap tap tap.

'Well, girls, d'you think we should give our new girl a treat for getting the best mark?'

'Yes, Sister,' they said.

I stood waiting, and Sister Felicity looked up at the clock behind her.

'Well now, why don't you entertain us for three minutes, on any subject you choose, starting . . .' She waited all that time for the second hand to touch twelve. '. . . now!'

Everything went into slow motion. Sister Felicity with that smug look on her face. The girls turned round in their chairs to look at me. I couldn't hear anything.

Then I snapped back into ordinary time and I was breathing fast and my heart was beating. The palms of my hands were sweaty, and I was holding on to the edge of my desk. Sister Felicity was still tapping the board pen. Those satisfied lips. She knew I couldn't even read in class without stammering. I kept opening my mouth but nothing came out. A chasm had opened up between me and words, any words, and my knees were trembling. Then my legs just collapsed under me and I sat down.

'Sorry, Sister,' I blurted. 'I can't.'

'Can't! Lower Five *love* this game! Come along, dear, I think you can do a bit better than that, can't she, girls?'

There was a low mumble.

'Yes, Sister.'

But I shook my head.

'Sorry, Sister.'

Sister Felicity turned hurriedly to Piggy.

'Come along, Pamela, stand up. I think we need to show our new girl not to be so easily defeated, and I'm sure that YOU can entertain us. Three munutes starting . . . now.'

But Piggy was the wrong girl to pick. She stood up and stared at Sister Felicity, and said not one word. The class was spellbound. The second hand moved slowly round the clock.

Something was slipping from Sister Felicity's grasp. I could tell she knew it from a flinch under her eye.

'Oh you really are rather hopeless. Sit down,' she said in her all-in-good-fun voice. 'Natalie, dear, stand up. I'm sure you will do better – you have such a wealth of experience from all the beautiful places you have travelled, not to mention your recent unfortunate experience.'

She gave Natalie a lead in, and it's true Natalie wants to please the nuns, but by now there was a strong force in the room. It willed her to say nothing, and she said nothing.

And after the bell rang for end of class, and Sister Felicity stepped off the wooden platform pretending not to notice she had been conquered, biting down a hidden rage between her teeth, all the girls who clambered past my desk patted me on the back, and said, 'Well done, Cath.'

And today the voices of the Upper School choir make sounds so beautiful they travel right through the heavy ceiling of the chapel into the darkening sky and out into the universe of multicoloured suns.

'But who heard it. Did you?'

'Yes, I did.'

'Oh come off it – you don't even sleep in Blue D.'

'Tessa's in the next-door cubicle.'

'Where is she?'

Everyone is talking at the same time, leaning over their breakfast trays.

There was a commotion last night in Blue D. The girls who sleep there were woken by loud whisperings and told to get back into bed at once when they poked their heads round the curtains of their cubicles. The light had come on and someone said they heard the voice of a man.

'Was it Father Finnigan?'

'No, it was a deep voice.'

'What was a man doing in Blue D?'

'Are you sure it wasn't Sister Scholastica?'

'No, it was a *man*.'

Tessa comes to our table with her tray.

Everyone looks at her expectantly, and pulls their chairs in close. She sits down and begins in a breathless whisper.

'You'll never guess what happened.'

And everyone leans in closer.

'Oh it's really awful.'

No one says, 'What?' but we allow her this moment of utter suspense when we are all hanging on her every breath.

'It really is awful.'

'What?' Lucy just can't help herself.

Tessa puts two strands of hair behind each ear, preparing for the speech, and pulls her chair in. She looks around at everyone.

'Fenella took all the Valium last night.'

Everyone gasps.

'All of them?'

'Is she still alive?'

'She had ten!'

'That's enough to kill a horse.'

'Rubbish – how do you know?'

'Well, not all of them. She must have been trying out the Coca-Cola thing. They had to pump out her stomach.'

'Oh please,' says Pen, looking down at her Redy-Brek.

'What Coca-Cola thing?' says Lucy.

'The doctor had to come at midnight.'

'The man's voice!' says Mouse.

'Ethelbug didn't know what to do – I heard it all through the partition. They came and took her away. I saw it through the crack in the curtain. She was wrapped up in a sheet and they carried her out. I don't know where they took her, probably the infirmary. She was all floppy. I thought she was dead!' says Tessa and bursts into tears.

Mouse puts her arm round to comfort her.

'She's not, though, Tess, it's all right.'

Tessa wipes her eyes, and recovers herself.

'No, she's OK – I heard the nuns talking. I asked Sister Campion this morning because I'm in the next-door cubicle so she said she could tell me. She said Fenella will be "right as rain".'

Everyone breathes a sigh of relief.

Sister Campion stands on the classroom platform holding a ruler and waiting for everyone to sit down at their desks.

She is going to talk to us before lessons because of what happened to Fenella.

She looks down at the ruler she is holding and then allows a silence to fall now that everyone is seated.

'As you know, Lower Four, there was an unfortunate incident last night in Blue D. I'm sure by now you know all about it and I don't need to furnish you with the details.

'Only one of Fenella's parents is Catholic, her father, and this can present some difficulties for a child. We know that there has been trouble at home, which has no doubt led to this call for attention.'

'What trouble at home?' Lucy whispers to Hen in the desk in front.

'How should I know,' whispers Hen.

'As we all know, if we read our doctrine, when God sends you any cross, or sickness, or pain, you should say, "Lord, your will be done, I take this for my sins,"' continues Sister Campion.

'Will she miss Function Day?' whispers Lucy.

'I don't *know*,' whispers Hen.

'And recently we had an excellent example of this in Natalie's behaviour when she was taken ill. I'm sure not one of you has heard a single word of complaint.'

Natalie blushes with due modesty and everyone wishes they had a twisted gut to show off how uncomplaining they could be, given the chance.

'After classes we will all go to chapel, together with Lower Four Remove, and offer up prayers for Fenella. She may not be shown a good example at home, so we must not judge, but look on this foolish act with compassion and patience.'

'Do the nuns think she wanted to, you know, kill herself?' whispers Lucy.

'Oh Lucy, how should I know what the nuns think. Why don't you ask Sister Campion?'

After tea Lower Four and Lower Four Remove line up outside the refectory for our visit to the chapel to offer up prayers for Fenella and her non-Catholic mother.

We file into the chapel in silence with Sister Campion at the front and Sister Scholastica, Remove's form mistress, at the back and sit down in the pews.

Fenella's action sits like a stone on my mind. I can't see through it, or round it.

The chapel is full of quietness, and the heavy stone.

Then the stone splits open and light shines through the crack. It illuminates the girls sitting in the rows in front and for a moment I see underneath. Under the bravado, the bitching, and the best friendships, coming first or last in class, and who's good at games, they are all like children sent to bed and crying in the dark, hoping it's not their fault. I never knew it before, I'd never seen it. I thought they were different from me, and for a reason I don't understand I burst into tears.

I feel a cool hand on mine, the storm has passed and I feel tired. I look up and Sister Campion motions for me to follow her out of the chapel.

We walk through the chapel doors and into the alcove where a candle is burning underneath the statue of Saint Anthony, the patron of lost things.

Sister Campion takes my hand and speaks gently.

'Catherine, dear, you are now at an age when all your feelings and reactions are exaggerated. Tiny things seem enormous and your world is out of proportion. This is also true for Fenella,' she says with a warning look, and pats my hand.

'But there's no need to draw attention to yourself. Fenella was no particular friend of yours. You must control yourself. You are one of the oldest girls in the class. You came to us late. So it's up to you to show a good example. Histrionics are no help to anyone. Now you may come back into the chapel if you think your behaviour will be appropriate.'

I nod, ashamed of my outburst, follow her back into the chapel, and return to my pew.

I couldn't explain to her that I wasn't crying for Fenella, that a light had shone through a cracked rock and lit up a hidden world that was so sad it had made me cry.

There's no point in saying things like that to nuns. It would be impertinent, which means 'not to the point'. Very told me that.

'That's codeine and it doesn't work any more.'

'Why?'

'They took the chemical out of Coca-Cola, so it doesn't make you high. Is she nice?'

'Don't really know her.'

'Sounds like she just wanted to get out of it.'

'Out of HERE, we all do.'

'You all right, Cat? You sound all quiet.'

'Oh don't worry, tell me stuff. How's Tracy?'

'Now I'm really worried.'

'Well, Eddie then, how's Eddie?'

'He's OK. You're not going to do something daft, are you?'

'What, you mean like eating Grip-fix?'

Very laughs. She's the one who eats Grip-fix.

'It's just you sound all faded and far away.'

'Don't say that, it makes me feel worse.'

'I'm going to take you out!'

'What?'

'Yes. I'm going to take you out. For the weekend.'

'You can't, Very. It's not . . . you can't.'

'Leave it to me. I'll work something out.'

'But, Very . . .'

'No, you need to get out, I can tell. You're all going mad. Twisted gut, overdose, no. Leave it to me. Got to go now, Cat.'

I put down the phone with a mixture of exhilaration and terror. Very is Very: she means what she says. I go and sit in the chapel to get some peace.

I see the first sign of something strange when Sister Campion looks at me with her head on one side and sorrowful eyes. She corners me on the way to the tea-urn, and beckons me into the alcove.

'Our prayers are with you, my dear, at this sad time. You were quite right to go straight to chapel to offer up prayers, but you do not need to bear the burden of bereavement alone.'

She accompanies me to Mother Agatha's office, talk-

ing about our cross and everything, and I listen atten-
tively, desperately trying to work out who Very said had
died. We don't have to wait at the lights, but go straight
in.

Mother Agatha stands up and walks round her desk
and sits in the chair next to me. The two nuns nod
at each other like conspirators and Sister Campion
leaves.

'I understand that your sister told you of the sad event
last night, and Sister Campion said you went straight to
the chapel.'

It makes me shiver how they know.

'I'm sure Sister Campion has told you that already we
have offered up our prayers.'

Who, though? Who did Very say?

I nod and mumble my gratitude.

'It is hard to bear, but remember, my child, God sees
all things, and knows all things.'

The colour must drain from my face because Mother
Agatha puts her cold hand on mine and says, 'There
now.'

'Yes, Mother.'

'So. Let us be practical. Sister Aloysius can accompany
you as far as Reading. Your sister will meet you at the
station.'

'When . . .' I say in a cracked voice.

'This afternoon, dear, naturally. You will leave in one
hour. You must hurry upstairs and pack at once. It is very
short notice for a funeral but understandable under the
circumstances,' she says in a low voice.

I walk up the creaking stairs to Yellow D, trembling with the excitement of leaving, and the terror of the deceit.

Before long I am sitting next to Sister Aloysius, thundering towards Very, feeling like an escaped convict, sure I'm going to get caught, and praying for Reading, because I still don't know who is supposed to have died.

When Reading has come and gone and little Sister Aloysius has edged her wide-beamed hips sideways down the aisle, and well and truly got off the train, and I know that nothing can stop it now, that I'm free till Sunday night, I can't stop smiling.

Everything looks beautiful, even the old coffee cup with a lipstick mark the lady opposite left on the table, and the passing landscape of industrial-storage warehouses.

We screech into King's Cross and Very appears standing outside the window of the carriage, knocking and smiling through her straggly hair, and her green eyes are lit up. She is dressed in a white shirt covered in paint-spots and a pair of blue-checked trousers that have paint-striped thighs. I jump off the train and carry on jumping because I can't stay on the ground.

We both start giggling because we've pulled it off, and I'm here and it was easy.

I'm so overjoyed to see her that I am halfway down Gower Street before I even notice my surroundings. I take huge steps along the pavement in the winter sunshine.

She's taking me to college.

'You can join in life drawing.'

'What about the teacher?'

'Oh he's in a world of his own – he won't notice.'

'Very, I'm supposed to be at games!' I say, and yelp. She laughs. I can't stop skipping.

'You'll meet Winnie. You'll like Winnie.'

We walk through the gates – Very says, 'Hi Bob,' to the gatekeeper – and into a huge quadrangle, where there is a lawn and a tree and great buildings on three sides. We cross the grass and walk up the stone steps into a cool high-ceilinged hall with grey walls and up more stairs on to a landing with tall windows that look on to the quadrangle and students lounging on the windowsills sipping hot drinks from polystyrene cups, dressed in paint-spattered dungarees and messy clothes, and every-one has dirty fingers.

She puts money in a machine and gets us thin black coffee and we sit on the windowsill in the sunlight.

'That's Old George,' says Very, answering a question I asked her weeks ago, pointing out of the window at a man in a grey suit and a white scarf with silver fringes, putting on a dark-blue coat. A man says something to him as he passes and Old George moves his head in a sideways motion that reminds me of the terrapin on the mantelpiece.

'He's like a lizard.'

Very laughs.

'It must be the grey suit,' she says.

But I think it's the long tail I see flicking out of the back of his coat as he walks away towards the gates.

Someone is playing a tape recorder and it sings, 'London calling from far away' and the haunting song echoes along the stone corridors and follows us down the dark-blue passage that opens into a large white room with tall windows that look out on to another green lawn. The room is empty but there is a circle of easels placed around an empty chair draped in scarlet velveteen with two foot shapes scratched in pink chalk where the feet should be.

'You can have this one,' says Very, pulling from the corner an easel that looks like a gangly giraffe. I wrestle with its splayed legs and wobbly neck trying to get it to stand at a proper angle and hold the drawing board straight. But there are so many nuts to tighten and screws to loosen that either it falls over as my precariously balanced drawing board falls off or leans so far backwards I can't tape my paper on the board. So Very has to help and between us we manage to make it stand straight.

The sunlight falls in squares on the paint-spattered floor and a line of charcoal dust collects beneath the easels. The room fills with scratching sounds and an absorbed concentration.

The stooped teacher has wobbly lips and spits all over the page. I draw Winnie's white shoulders and breasts and long hands. It's not until she stands up that I am amazed to see she has a penis, and I wonder how it was I didn't notice.

'It's from Hermes and Aphrodite, I'm a double deity,' says Winnie. She's sitting on a chair in her satin dressing gown from Chinatown with her feet up on a stool.

'Two for the price of one,' says Eddie, who's just arrived with two bacon rolls, which we're all sharing.

'You should be so lucky,' says Winnie, unscrewing her nail polish and leaning over to paint her toenails.

We sit in Very's cramped space amid the easels and propped-up canvases with charcoal drawings and postcards taped all over the hardboard partitions. Eddie leans against the grey radiator that keeps clunking, and lights a cigarette.

'What time does it start?' he says.

'Well, I'm on at nine,' says Winnie, delicately touching his heart.

Very is standing in the corner drawing everyone with a frown on her face and intent eyes that look piercingly at you and back at her book.

'I thought Tracy was coming,' Winnie says in a sad voice. 'She told me she'd come.'

'Oh she's so full of herself these days.'

'Well, why shouldn't she be.'

'She's played two gigs at a poxy pub in Hoxton and now she's a star.'

'Well, they got a write-up in the *NME*.'

'Oh so what,' says Eddie, stubbing out his cigarette in the blue Tennant's lager ashtray on Very's table.

'Ooh,' says Winnie, raising her eyebrows.

Eddie shifts and pouts, then gives way to a resentful smile.

It's hard to be offended by Winnie – he's so gentle and soft. He has high cheekbones and sweet loving eyes.

'I don't want her to come if she brings Brainy,' says Winnie, blowing on her nails.

'Oh-oh, she's got that knife-and-fork look on her face.' says Eddie, nodding at Very.

Very has her jaw clenched. She's fighting with her drawing. You can say her name but she doesn't hear you. She's in her drawing world.

'D'you think we should wake her from her trance? VERY!'

She looks up.

'It's not that important.'

Very looks down at her drawing and sighs through flared nostrils.

'It's all right,' says Eddie, as though he's humouring a madman. 'It's only a drawing.'

He turns to us, and mouths 'Sometimes she forgets' then he prises the book away. 'That's enough for today. It's time to put the straitjacket back on. Don't worry, you won't feel a thing. Me and my assistant here,' he nudges Winnie, 'are just going to give you a little sedative.'

Winnie starts giggling.

Very sighs, gives in and seems to wake up from her dream.

'So are you singing tonight, Winnie?'

'Oh let's just have all the conversations we've just had now the loony's woken up,' says Eddie.

'Yes I am,' says Winnie shyly.

The windows in the roof that flood the room with light from the sky are turning blue and we sit in the dimming dusk. I watch Eddie's cigarette glow red, lighting his face when he takes a puff. The air seems to be filled with gentle voices like in a wood, and I wonder if it is the sound of all the ideas ready to fall out of the space near the ceiling and into the students' minds.

We walk out of the gates wrapped up in our coats with our arms folded against the cold.

'Bye, Bob,' says Very.

'Bye, Very.'

We walk along the road past the tall, dark-red-stone hospital and into Tottenham Court Road and the rushing people, past the lit-up letters flashing in the windows.

A man in a shop doorway is selling expensive perfume for next to nothing, and gold chains at bargain prices. He holds them out to Very then says, 'Sorry, guv, thought you was a girl,' and offers them to Winnie.

The evening is full of noises, tooting and sirens, tramping feet and swishing wheels.

I follow Winnie's black-and-white boots through the crowds. I keep my eyes on the white stripe down the back. It changes colour in the reflected neon signs.

*   *   *

The dressing room at Madame Fifi's smells of different perfumes, and the greasy cream they wipe their faces with before they put on the powder. Very calls it slap. She is sitting in the corner next to the rail of glittering dresses, different-coloured sequins and stiff net frills. There are feather boas and gauze underskirts and slinky gold-and-silver-sequin dresses. Very is sitting on the huge armchair drawing feverishly as the girls sit and stand at the mirrors applying their slap and powder with pink fluffy powder puffs, then red lipstick, pink lipstick, pearly purple lipstick. They are all men dressing up as women except Winnie who is both.

A man with plucked eyebrows and no hair is putting on his false eyelashes. He has a long scraggy neck and beak nose that make him look like an emu.

He catches sight of me looking, in the mirror.

'I know,' he says to my reflection, 'an emu,' and I burst out laughing.

He beckons me over and puts pale-blue glittering eyeshadow on my eyelids but I have to refuse the pearlescent lipstick because it reminds me of Miss Bolt.

Very is sitting sideways with her legs flung over the arm, drawing rapidly. They cast her sidelong glances as they draw black lines under their eyelids or bend down to hitch up their stockings to see if she is drawing them.

The man with big biceps squashed into a red satin corset is called Juliet.

Eddie refuses to come backstage.

'Who on earth wants to be a girl. You wouldn't catch me in a bloody frock.'

We join him at a round table in front of the miniature stage that has a pale-blue circle of light shining on to the curtain of silver ribbons. He is puffing away into the smoky atmosphere, and looking people up and down.

He presses his fingers to his cheeks and shakes his head.

'What some people wear! It's BEYOND me!'

And Very sits down beside him and says. 'You don't mind what I wear.'

'Darling, you have entirely your own style. I wouldn't criticise it any more than I would a freak, sorry, a force of nature.'

Very snorts and hits him.

'Why don't you wear a dress now and then, Very?'

Very shrugs.

'I feel like I'm in drag,' and they both laugh.

A man in a suit and a very big red handkerchief in his pocket steps through the curtain of silver ribbons and into the circle of blue light which turns yellow. He adjusts the microphone and clears his throat.

'Ladies and gentlemen, we have a lovely line-up of ladies for you tonight so put your hands together and welcome the slinky Samantha.'

An enormous blonde in pale-lemon sequins steps through the curtain on lemon stilettos and takes the mike. A tune starts up and she mimes 'Ooh love to love you, baby' and a song about a cake being left out in the rain so she has to bake another one, and everyone claps.

Winnie comes on in green sequins, looking like a mermaid, and we all shout compliments. Winnie doesn't mime. She sings in her own voice 'Where Have All the Flowers Gone?' in German and it makes tears come to my eyes though I don't understand one word except for *Blumen*.

In the sitting room in Very's flat is a pile of *National Geographics* with dog-eared yellow covers. You have to be careful if you want to read them because the stack is making up for two missing legs on the low table where she puts the jars of turpentine and rabbit-skin glue and goodness knows what because it smells disgusting and grows mould. But sometimes you have to, if you want to see the pink flamingos who live in the piping-hot soda lakes. We read the magazines out loud to each other in the bath and some of the copies are crinkled after falling in. So when Winnie says, 'A few of the girls are going up to the Angel to see *Pink Flamingos* – it's on Late Night at the Screen,' I say, 'Come on, Very, let's go.'

'Are you sure you want to go, Cat?'

'Yes, please, Very, let's.'

So we wait outside the stage door next to the dustbins that smell of rotting vegetables and the alley is dark and quiet. The girls pile out of the back door as though they're tied together with string and all talking at once, squawking and laughing loudly. They glitter in the dark alley.

The streets of Soho are brightly lit and the crowd of men dressed as women calls whistling out of the shadows. We walk towards Tottenham Court Road in the wet sparkling London night and the sky is purple with orange clouds.

Very puts her arm in mine.

'How's Olive?'

'She's fine.'

'Tell me one of her facts.'

I look in my pocket and hand a coin to Very.

'Stretch out your arm.'

Very stretches out her arm.

'Find a space in the sky as big as the coin, and even if it looks empty you would find at least five hundred thousand galaxies in that little space, if you had a telescope strong enough. I'm not saying stars, Very, I'm saying galaxies!'

Very shakes her head and blows her fringe upwards.

'Phew!' she says, and gives me back the coin.

Juliet and his wife clip along the wet pavement arm in arm, avoiding the puddles, each carrying the same handbag.

Very suddenly shouts, 'Thirty-eight!' and we all run across the road in a crowd that stops the traffic, and a man rolls down his window and shouts, 'Bloody trannies,' and someone else shouts, 'Go for it, girls.'

We clamber on to the top deck and sit at the front so we can see the glittering night and when we pass by King's Cross everyone cranes their necks and looks through my window, because a police car has stopped and its blue light is flashing, lighting up the girls' powdered, stubbled faces in a rhythm, and the policemen are bundling a woman into the back seat but someone else is running, and a policeman takes his hat off and chases after, and everyone shouts for them to get away.

I am a bit disappointed by the tall dark buildings and black crossroads, where we get out 'quickly! or it'll take us down Essex Road'. I had pictured a different Angel. And *Pink Flamingos* turns out to be a film that has no rating ('What does that mean, Very?' 'It means it's worse than double X'), so we have to write our names in a book.

I write 'Lavinia Stowe', my table-head.

We sit in the very front row under the screen and one of the girls opens her handbag and takes out lollipops. She holds them in her hand like a fan, orange, lime, lemon and red, and hands them round.

The film is about Divine, a man with an egg-shaped head and surprised painted eyebrows. People keep walking across a muddy field to visit each other in their caravans. Divine eats dog shit off the pavement and everyone argues about whether he really did it. Juliet's wife hands round a joint and clouds of blue fragrant smoke rise into the air. The film disappears and everything becomes funny. The front row collapses in hysterics. Juliet slides out of her chair so her wig falls off and everyone is in stitches.

We laugh at everything. We don't even know why we are laughing. We laugh at each other laughing. We laugh till we cry. People are on their knees on the floor with their skirts riding up their thighs, crawling along the flickering carpet. I get the hiccups, then Very gets the hiccups too, and they sound like saucepans clanging together and that makes us laugh more. The funniness of everything fills the dark cinema and flows over the lit-up Exit sign, and the flickering faces watching the film. It bounces off the wigs on the girls' shadowed heads and reflects off their glinting nails and sparkly eyelids and ripples through the smoky auditorium tickling us and making us ache till Very and I are doubled over holding our stomachs and helplessly calling, 'Stop!'

Then Very sighs and sits back. The tear-streams down her cheeks flicker in the film's light.

The laughing explodes and shrinks and suddenly nothing is funny, my eyes hurt, and I think, I was at early Mass this morning, and fall asleep on Very's shoulder.

When she shakes me awake, the lights are on, someone is picking up rubbish into a black sack and the girls are looking for their handbags with smudged eyes.

Very and I catch the N19 from St John Street, through the dark, lit-up city, and when we arrive home the birds are singing in the square.

'I'd like to see him flattened under a truck! He's so mean he hides his silver away in a plastic bag. "Bury it for me, McGonogall," he says. "I'll do no such thing," I says. "And my name is Mary or Miss McGonogall to you." Then I say, "I've put it in the bin," to tease him, "and the dustbin men'll carry it off," and I laugh. He goes pale, paler than he is, because look at him now, he's almost dead, and I think to myself this'll kill him. If I tease him long enough his heart is sure to stop.'

She coughs a long hard cough and pats her chest with bent arthritic fingers.

'Oh my lungs aren't good. But there now, reach the tin down for me, and what a beautiful young girl you are – your mother is sure to be proud of you. Is she proud of you? I bet she is. He's a mean old bugger. He shouts down the stairs to me, "Mary," he shouts, "Mary, come here," as though I'm his slave just here to serve him,' and she unscrews her old tin from Ireland where she grew up and hands me a biscuit. 'Here, darling, have a biscuit, they're fresh. Oh I'll kill 'im one day. I'll find a way,' she says, and smiles me a creased warm smile from her little yellow face with eyes as bright and clear as a child's. 'There's a bit of me in that eggnog,' she says. 'I've put a bit of me in there especially for you.'

And I wish she hadn't said that because something soft and floating is bumping against my lip when I sip the thick concoction, and it's probably a bit of egg not mixed in but it could easily be a bit of Mrs McGonogall that she put in there especially for me.

'It'll perk you up,' she said.

It's terrible how one thing leads to another if you can't say no. One minute you're looking down the street watching Very walk towards the bus stop to go to the club where Eddie's found her a job checking coats from six till three in the morning, and the next thing you know you're being tapped on the shoulder by a long arm, and beckoned by a yellow finger through a dark doorway that leads downwards, and before you know it you're sitting in a basement that smells of old gravy, drinking eggnog with a bit of Mrs McGonogall bumping against your lip.

We'd got up so late that I just lay in my pyjamas being painted by Very until it was time for her to go, and she left the canvas on the easel and all the paint on the palate.

'Do some painting if you like,' Very said when she put on a donkey jacket and pulled the collar up against the wind. 'And if you get lonely . . .'

'No, I'm not visiting Mrs McGonogall.'

But when it came to it I couldn't say no at the important moment.

'Oh my back's not good, dearie me,' she says, holding her back. 'Look how tall I'd be! See the length of these arms? And I have big hands,' she says, stretching out her arms and fingers, and I see she is right because they are far longer than mine while she only reaches up to my shoulder.

'At least you didn't die when you fell out,' I say. 'At least you're alive.'

'Alive!' she says. 'Alive! Some life! I'm not afraid of dying, though,' she says, 'but HE is!' And she points at the ceiling with her knife and her eyes flick up. 'He's terrified! But more scared of losing his silver. Oh I'll give him the fright of his life one day, tell him it's been took, and he'll drop dead on the spot,' and her eyes twinkle in her wizened yellow face. 'Oh no, I had a back as straight as an arrow!' she says, climbing off her chair to open another biscuit tin, and pulls out a photograph and hands it to me.

'Eat up your biscuit now, don't let it go to waste.'

I look at the browned photograph of the bright-eyed child with a defiant stare and a back as straight as an arrow, who was always climbing trees no matter how many times she was told, 'You'll fall out one day, you'll fall out and break your back!' and that was exactly what happened. It was her big sister Edith who always used to scold her, and *she* was gifted with the sight, it was said, but Mary said it was a lie, that Edith was a witch and had jinxed her out of the tree to serve her right. Edith grew up and turned religious because of the guilt.

Suddenly there is a loud thudding on the ceiling and Mary clenches her teeth and looks up.

'What does the old bugger want now?'

She climbs off her stool and clambers up the stairs, wheezing. When she opens the door at the top a loud voice growls through the crack. It makes my hair stand on end.

Mary slams the door and clambers back down the stairs.

'He wants to get up!' she says, exasperated. 'It's half-past six in the evening, but HE wants to get up! He's just being awkward. He does it to annoy me!'

'What did you tell him?'

'I told him if he wants to get up and get his clothes on he can do it his bloody self! I'm paid as a housekeeper, not a nanny!'

'Oh is that really the time?' I say, leaving my congealing egg concoction in the low square sink.

'I'd better get back upstairs. Dear me – I had no idea it was so late. Thank you for the eggnog, Mrs McGonogall.'

'Miss! And it's Mary to you!'

'Thank you,' I say again, walking backwards up the stairs with Mary following behind.

'Come any time – I can cook you a bit of stew,' she says.

'Yes, thank you,' I say again and close the door, as another growl roars out of the old man's bedroom.

I run up the stairs and into the flat and fall on to the dark-brown sofa with relief and smell the turpentine and cigarettes. Then I sit down on the floor to paint a picture of the street light and the dark-blue sky. But I keep thinking of Mary McGonogall and the street light turns into a tree and a small figure falls out of the blue paint with all its limbs pointing upwards.

In the daylight I am disappointed. I had been happy with the result last night and wanted to show it to Very, but now the colours are garish and ugly.

And this morning is the morning of the day that I go back, and it's one o'clock and I've been awake since eight, banging up and down the stairs in the hope of rousing Very, but she's been lying diagonally across the bed with her arms outstretched and that hungry-for-sleep look on her face, for the last five hours.

The telephone rings and I sit on the stairs hoping it will wake her. She stumbles out of the bedroom and I can tell she's still asleep because she says, 'I think it's on the shelf,' to the telephone when she picks it up, instead of 'Hello', and I walk into the sitting room to listen. Then she wakes up and says, 'Oh . . . mmm . . . OK . . . yeah . . . bye,' and puts the phone down.

'Who was that?'

'Old George,' she says.

'Oh? What did he want?'

'Go out to lunch,' says Very, yawning and rubbing her head.

'What, today?'

'Yeah.'

'Are you going to go?'

'Yeah, I just said yeah.'

A great chasm opens under my feet. I've waited all this time for her to wake up, it's my last day, I have to go back at teatime and she's going on a date without me. I knock down the easel on purpose and run out of the room not caring if my painting has landed face down on the carpet, and run up the stairs into the bathroom, lock the door, sit down on the loo and burst into tears.

Very comes thumping up the stairs and bangs on the door.

'What's wrong, Cath? Open the door . . . Come on, open it!'

I have to stand in the bath to open the door, and Very has to stand in the bath to shut it.

'What on earth is wrong?'

We are both standing in the bath.

'It's my last day, I have to go back,' I scream, 'and you're going out on a date with some bloody old man for lunch.'

'But, Cat, you're coming too, you stupid idiot.'

'Am I?' I say weakly.

'Nit-wit! What d'you think I'm going to do – leave you on your own on your last day, you big twit!' and we both climb out of the bath and go back downstairs.

A huge blue car slides up outside the door in the street below.

'Is that it?'

'Yep,' says Very.

His blue eyes dart towards me and he nods. I get in the back and we slide off, and he tells Very about New York and how dangerous it is, because there are mad people who lie on the top of buildings with guns and shoot every third person with yellow socks, and I look out the window thinking, well, I'd never get killed. Come to think of it, who would? And I scour the pavements all the way to the restaurant and don't count one person with yellow socks. He'll be up there for weeks and probably die of cold.

The restaurant is green with gold letters and there is a carpet on the floor and we are shown to the table by waiters who pull out the chairs with soft padded backs, and don't bat an eyelid at Very's wellingtons. The thick white napkins are folded into pyramids and there is a hushed feeling in the air that smells of fish.

We have oysters that arrive in their crusted shells, and Old George shows us how to eat them. Prise them open, lean back and swallow the quivering animal whole so the trail of sea taste makes you almost hear the waves, and

Old George swivels his eyes and slides them up and down the curtains.

We each have a different fish and mine is thin and yellow with white flesh that comes apart in soft flakes. And Very and Old George speak in low voices and smile at me and sometimes write a note to each other in Very's sketch book.

The meal is delicious, and we have coffee and thin mint chocolates. But when Old George drops us outside the wrong station and the long blue car drives away and neither of us notice till we're left stranded outside Euston instead of King's Cross, in a wind full of dust and sweetie papers, and we have to run along the Euston Road, I feel that the lunch deceived me. I should have been preparing for this moment of horrible gloom when dread clutches me and invisible insects come alive, clawing and shuddering in the space around.

And then I hate everything. I hate the brown London night and the yellow street light and the glowing faces of the pale girls with dark lips and the bristly chin and toothless sneer of the man slumped in the glass door of a closed shop shouting swear words to nobody. I hate the hurrying people and the smell of oil and smoke and the dirty buildings and the cans and packets and see-through plastic paper and empty cigarette packets that are blown into the corners of the street by the dust-filled wind. And I hate the shouting people and the sad faces and the tramps sitting in rows in the station with plastic bags and nowhere else to go. I hate the tall ceiling and the flicking names that tell the destination of the trains, and I have to keep my mouth shut in case I open it and all the hate comes out and I start shouting or screaming because Very is standing there holding my bag and she's leaving me here and walking off into her freedom, and I hate her too.

And then I'm in the train opposite an old lady and my bag is on the rack and I watch Very being left behind on the platform mouthing 'I'll write' and miming it, and I hate her so much I want to shout something vile, but the train is leaving, passing the metal columns, then the circular gas works, gathering speed and entering into the dark twilight. And the old lady opposite looks at me kindly but my hate-filled eyes slice her in two and she looks away.

But by the time the conductor announces my station the shell of hatred has split open and I am left on the dark station platform, small and quivering, and as I am driven through the gates, the convent looks like a big face, and the front doors are open, ready to swallow me.

PART FOUR

I walk up the steps and through the glass doors into the same smell of disinfectant and old food, on to the same grey lino under the too-bright lights that constantly flicker.

'Welcome back, dear. Was your train delayed? We were expecting you an hour ago.'

It is Sister Felicity with her fixed smile.

I mumble yes, or no, I can't tell which.

'We were sorry to hear of your grandmother's death,' she says, nodding.

'Thank you, Sister.'

At least she told me. I'd forgotten to ask Very who she said died. And I wonder how two days and two nights can pass in a flash of time. And I wonder why Sister Felicity's face seems too detailed, so I can see the pores on her nose and each black eyelash and eyebrow hair. And why do I see her mouth speaking in slow motion but no words coming out? Why do I have to blink and swallow to concentrate on what she has just said, only now the words are hanging in the air outside the gym door, so I have to step to the side to get close and hear what they say?

'Maternal, Sister. Maternal grandmother.'

'Your mother will be in our prayers.'

'Yes, Sister. Thank you, Sister.'

'Well, upstairs, dear, quickly, or you'll be there after lights out.'

A heavy feeling sinks in me as the school closes in, and I hurry up the stairs and along the darkened corridors.

Sister Gertrude has stick-like arms and wrists so thin you could snap them. Her intense, mad-smiling eyes look through me.

'Hurry along, dear, into bed.'

There are coughs and noises from behind the curtains. She whispers in a hiss, 'It's past time, no talking.'

I lie in my bed like a coffin and think about dead Granny, and a little moth of dread opens its wings and flutters in my ribs. I hope they don't find out Granny died when I was two.

I wake with a start. I'd been dreaming of bright colours and hot light, and trees that shed blue petals on the road. I lift the curtain and look at the grey sky. The electric morning bell shrieks down the corridor and is left ringing.

Tap-tap.

'God be with you.'

'God be with you, Sister.'

I pull back the covers and sit on the edge of the bed. I hear bumps and thuds from the next-door cubicle as Hen gets out of bed. The air is still ringing though the bell has been switched off. I can feel it trembling through my atoms. I pull back the curtain and spots of rain are hitting the window.

When I was asleep I was alive. But now I'm awake I try to activate my dead mind. Geography first lesson. Who cares.

I remember you could always tell when the rain was coming. It began with the warm winds in the night and the sound of the water drops hitting the leaves, quietly pattering and bouncing, and the rattling doors as the warm wind swept through the house. It would fall in a gentle rhythm for the rest of the night. And the next day the yellow road had dark streams. The water sank into the ground by breakfast, evaporated in the hot sun by the time we ran out of the house, up the hill and past the crying tree and the tethered donkeys, into the wood to see the crowns of yellow or pink flowers that burst out of the prickly heads of the cactus because of the delicious rain.

But the geography room is cold and the wind rattles the glass and moans along the gulley outside. We are in the basement. Only the top half of the window sees the grass stalks. We are in the cold ground, below the moles and the worms. Only bacteria and mould live this far down.

I gaze at the map of the world on the wall, at the thin strip of land that joins North and South America. From here it doesn't look three thousand miles long, and you can't see the huge hills sleeping in the heat or the jacaranda trees that drop their purple petals on the road. I remember the hot light and the red house and the courtyard full of climbing plants. In the shadows the walls were purple. I remember the road passed the orange tree. We used to collect the fruit with a long split stick. You had to aim for the stalk and pull, so the orange bounced on to the grass with the leaves still on.

'Pay attention – what have I written on the board?'

Sister Peter has eyes with droopy lids which slant upwards towards her nose, so she looks like a sleepy owl.

'New-town planning, Sister.'

I look back at the map.

The road led down the hill to the Corazón de Jesús pharmacy where women with pink ribbons plaited into their long grey hair sat weaving coloured baskets.

We were fascinated by the metal hearts, silver legs, hands and eyes that shook back and forth in the breeze making a gentle clicking sound, on the stall outside the dark cool church where old ladies hit each other with flowers in front of the glimmering saints.

That day we followed the road to the market in the outskirts of the sprawling city. We walked past the fruit stalls where the juicy scent of sliced-open mangos flavoured the air, past the flowers and the wasps, and the rotting vegetables, into the smell of sizzling fish and spicy *mole*. Past the *chilequile* stalls, *tortillas* and sweet cakes.

Sister Peter's green pen is running out and squeaking across the grey board, squeak squeak. We have plotted a graph, we have done a pie chart, and now we are listing points for the committee to take into consideration after the survey. The enlargement of the road, the precinct, the new shopping centre and pedestrian access.

Very led us out of the market into a labyrinth of steep dark alleyways that smelt of drains. We came out of the labyrinth and found ourselves in a different kind of place. Between the houses were trees where dogs lay asleep in the cool shade and flowerbeds where large cacti and flowers grew. Each house had a front door and a side alley and a little gulley ran along beside the path and water flowed along it and made a gurgling sound.

'It's here!' said Very, looking at a tattered piece of paper from her back pocket and up at the door.

And when we sneaked up the alley to spy through the slats we were astonished at what we saw.

'Pavements, street lights, take this down, please, car-parks, traffic signs and signals, zig-zag lines, where to put the zebra crossings, traffic islands, oval or round. Underground car-parks are a possibility.'

There is a huge bored sigh rising up from the classroom. Sister Peter tries the red pen but it's running out as well, squeak squeak squeak, and Piggy looks across at Hen and pats her open mouth.

'Now we can transfer our pie chart into a block-chart graph.'

'Aren't we lucky!' murmurs Hen.

When the red spiders scuttled across the ceiling and the house seemed gripped by a cold hand I wanted to tell Mummy that the lady wasn't like that. That she had a pretty smile and long lilac nails, that she didn't roast him or eat his entrails. But when I walked past her bedroom her eyelids flinched so painfully I never said a word.

'You can use two colours for the block-chart graph.'

'Two colours, Sister, that's wonderful!' says Eliza.

'You need some new pens, Sister.'

'Yes, Penelope, thank you for stating the obvious.'

The truth is Sister Peter is bored to death by new-town urban development. I can see from her tired expression and the way she sighs when she looks at the textbook. She wanted to be a missionary, Lavinia Stowe said, but then she got arthritis and they wouldn't let her go. So they gave her geography instead.

We tediously transform our pie charts into block-chart graphs using two colours.

'Are you sure she's a witch?' I asked Very, wishing I hadn't come.

'Yes, I heard Conchita say.'

'It's probably the wrong house.'

'No, this is the address.'

'It doesn't look like a witch's house, though.'

'How do you know?'

But we looked through the wooden slats at the window and saw a man standing on the stone floor in a heaped circle of white and yellow flowers and green herbs, while a small woman with long black hair tied him together with plaited ribbon.

'It's her.'

'What's she doing?'

'She's going to sacrifice him.'

He was standing motionless.

'Why doesn't he run away?'

'He's already under a spell,' said Very.

With her back to us the woman tied his hands and wrists and feet and legs, and then began to tie the ribbon round his head and neck.

'She's going to burn him,' said Very.

Then the witch stepped out of the circle and squeezed a squeezy bottle of clear liquid at the circle of flowers. She lit a match and threw it on to the flowers so they crackled and a pungent aromatic smoke rose up from the herbs and filled the room, and blew through the slats into our faces.

'She's roasting him,' said Very.

And my heart beat against my chest and I put my hands over my eyes and peeked through my fingers as the smoke cleared because I didn't want to see, but I couldn't look away.

'Now she'll eat him!' said Very.

She kept squeezing the bottle and lighting the circle when the flames died down. When the flowers and herbs were a pile of ash, to our surprise she stepped into the circle with a big pair of scissors and cut and snipped the ribbon till the man was free. She threw the pieces on the floor where she set them alight, then she rubbed the man all over with an egg, but the egg seemed to get dirty quickly because she kept using a new one.

When she gently helped him out of the circle and bent over the burnt remains of the ribbon to read the pictures they made, and when she wrapped his head in a scarf to protect his ears from the wind, I knew she wouldn't eat him, and when she kissed his cheek and hugged him goodbye and he went out the front door so we had to jam ourselves up against the wall so as not to be seen, I looked at Very and frowned. But she just scratched her cheek, covered her mouth with her hand, and laughed.

And it was Very herself who went and told Mummy that we'd been to spy on the witch, and that was the only time I ever saw Mummy angry.

The bell rings for the end of the lesson, and Sister Peter looks relieved as she closes her textbook. We walk in a file out of the classroom.

Maybe it was coincidence but, by the time the headache was gone, the talk began about Very's uniform, and when it was to be ordered for it to arrive in time, so it could be packed up and sent off like she was.

The next time I put my head under the curtain to look at the moon, Natalie is on the other side of the partition.

We give each other a shock.

She is kneeling on her bed in her nightie with her elbows on the windowsill.

'What are you doing?' I whisper.

'Dreaming of boys,' she says, and lays her head on her crossed arms and closes her eyes. Her face is lit up by the moonlight.

'There'll be loads of boys on Function Day,' she whispers.

'Will there?'

Natalie wants to fall in love with the right one and then she'll be able to wear the wedding dress she designs over and over again in the back of her rough book. He'll send her roses, and love letters, and hold her hand in the moonlight. It is a dream she carries with her. She takes it out and wraps it round her during study, and it throbs and moves like flower petals in a breeze.

She opens her eyes and looks at me.

'Are you feeling OK, I mean, after the funeral and everything?'

I can't bear the deceit. I have to tell someone.

'No one died, Natalie.'

'What?'

'My sister made it up so she could get me out for the weekend.'

'That's terrible!' says Natalie in a loud whisper.

'I know,' I say, 'it's really bad.'

'I wish I had a sister who did that.'

Suddenly we hear the rustle of a habit and the faint rattle of rosary beads. We close our mouths and look at each other, not daring to breathe. But the footsteps pass by, and we breathe out.

'D'you want to help me do the quiz?' Natalie asks.

I nod.

She disappears under the curtain and comes back with her *Jackie* magazine, and a pencil to keep score. The moon is bright enough to read by.

*   *   *

If you go to a party do you wear:
a) trousers
b) a skirt
c) a sparkly dress

When you're talking to a boy do you:
a) do all the talking
b) let him talk but look bored
c) gaze at him lovingly while he tells you about his new motorbike

Natalie knows all about boys and how to make them like you. She scores seventy-four, and I score six.

The morning of Function Day, the bell drings constantly the 'get-up' ring, and Sister Gobnet comes round tap-tapping on the wood.

'God be with you,' she says through the curtain.

'God be with you, Sister,' I answer.

Tap-tap.

'God be with you.'

But there is no answer from Henhouse on the other side.

'God be with you,' she repeats.

Sister Gobnet teaches hockey and musical appreciation. She always has a red face. I felt sorry for her until she emptied all my knickers on the bed and said, 'A tidy cupboard, a tidy mind,' on inspection day, and I asked her if she had a tidy mind and she gave me three conduct marks for insolence. I wasn't being insolent, I had really wanted to know if her mind was like a tidy cupboard with everything in the same place every day, and if it was, how did she get it like that. But she just gave me a furious maroon look and said, 'Three conduct marks.'

Henhouse is still snoring. I can hear Sister Gobnet pull back the curtain.

'God be with you, Sister,' she suddenly says too loud, finally roused out of sleep.

'I should think so too!' says Sister Gobnet.

Outside the sky is dark, and the dormitory is cold. I look at my shiny beige Function dress hanging on the cupboard. It will slide coldly over my skin and draw all the sleep heat from my body.

Everyone hates the Function dress. It has an A-line skirt that sticks out and the material pulls across the chest if you've got bosoms, or the darts stick out where your bosoms are supposed to be but aren't. I decide to do it quickly, like diving into a cold pool. I draw back the covers, pull off my nightie, scramble into my vest and pants, and slip the Function dress over my head.

But that's when I realise. The wide skirt slips over but the bodice is stuck above my bosoms. They must have grown in the night. My arms are sticking up in the air and all I can see is beige.

'Natalie,' I whisper through the wooden partition. 'Natalie!'

They weren't this big yesterday, I know they weren't.

'Natalie!' I whisper again.

Oh God, they're going to be as big as Camilla Bell's in Lower Five by the time I get to Upper School.

I knock on the wood with my elbow.

'Natalie, I'm stuck!'

'Wait a minute,' says Natalie through the partition. 'I'm coming.'

I hear her pull the curtain back. She starts giggling.

'What have you done?'

'It's not funny, Natalie, I'm stuck.' My face is heating up and I'm beginning to panic.

'Wait,' she says, 'I know what to do.'

She yanks the skirt down and pulls the bodice over my chest but then I can't breathe.

'No,' I squeak, 'Natalie.'

'It's OK, it's OK,' she says.

She pulls it up the other way, and I hear a rip as I breathe out. I manage to struggle free and Natalie fetches her scissors and undoes the sewing under the arms. She tells me to keep my cardigan on no matter what but the dress still pulls across the chest when I put it back on, a lopsided crease from one bosom to the other.

'I can't go downstairs like this!'

'Yes, you can.'

So I go downstairs and stand in the breakfast queue and try to make crossing my arms over my chest look normal.

Everyone was chattering like anything at breakfast, because it's Function Day and who's coming and who is going to win which cup. Piggy said there should be a cup for being a new girl and surviving your first term, and everyone laughed and I was glad.

And when we went back upstairs after breakfast Natalie and I got the giggles, because she'd seen me in the breakfast queue.

'At least you've got some!' she'd said, opening her cardigan. 'Where are mine?' And we'd both started giggling again.

And now I'm scratching a spider's web on my green rough book with my mouth tight shut, joining the red dots I drew yesterday and turning the moon into a spider. Because Sister Campion had to go and spoil it all. I keep looking at Natalie sitting at the desk by the window. But it won't make any difference.

The fountain pen leaks by the gold italic nib. I can smell the ink on my finger. I blot it on the page – it's what the police do when you've committed a crime. Very told me that's why they wear gloves and I imagine Big Terry climbing in a window with his leather gloves on and his coat squeaking, but Very says he's not the one who does the crimes any more. You have to sit for a mug shot, front and side view.

Natalie and I were the first two. We'd run down the stairs from Yellow D. The stairwells smelt of polish and the steps stuck to the soles of our shoes.

Natalie was so excited because today we'd see boys.

Now she's looking out of the window trying to keep her bottom lip straight but there's that wobble in her chin. She'd put the yellow daisy in her hair.

'That's nice,' I'd said.

'I know,' she'd said. 'I've got a pink one too.'

She'd washed her hair last night. She told me about

conditioner. I'd never heard of it. It got the tangles out and made the hair shine.

'See?' she said, 'it's shiny.'

I agreed it was shiny. She picked up the ends, 'But split ends,' she'd said, and sighed.

I hadn't heard of split ends either.

And we'd walked under Sister Campion's tall wooden desk, first into the classroom and out of breath.

Sister Campion had said it quickly in a cutting, icy voice. She'd leaned over her desk as Natalie passed.

'Oh Natalie, you DO love yourself this morning!' Then turned to the door and called, 'Come along, girls!' in another voice.

Natalie had stood still and reached up to her hair, to the yellow daisy, hoping the cold in Sister's voice was a joke.

But Sister Campion kept looking at the door, and the sight of Natalie touching the yellow flower and smiling at Sister Campion, desperately, with tears in her throat even when Sister Campion was looking the other way made me want to cry too.

So I sit at my desk while Natalie sits by the window trying to control her face and make blue fingerprints on the back page of my rough book because no two people have fingerprints the same, and wonder what is wrong with putting a flower in your hair and loving yourself this morning.

Gawky flower arrangements have appeared on tables in the refectory, on the Upper School lockers by the chemistry lab, outside Mother Agatha's office, and on the stage in the gym, where the bazaar is being held.

The wobbly trestle tables are covered with yellow crêpe paper, and set up on the squeaking wooden floor. There is a food stall with see-through packets of fudge and trays of shortcake made by the Lower Five domestic science, the haberdashery stall with handkerchief-box covers made of spotted muslin by Upper Four needle-work. Everyone is crooning over the Junior School's holy cards of large-eyed infants with haloes. A second-hand stall is the centre and prize attraction.

'If you want to be a prefect in the Upper School you'd better start bringing good stuff for the bring-and-buy when you're still in Lower School.' That's what Eliza says.

We lean against the stage and wait for each girl's family to arrive, and watch as she slips into a small group of people who all look a bit like her.

Suddenly the nose from Upper Four that is similar to the nose in Junior School and in Lower Five all come together as sisters, with the father, the source of the nose. A Lower Six has a miniature in Third Form, and they are both miniatures of their mother. I am glad when Natalie's elegant French mother arrives, and brushes Natalie's hair back from her forehead in a mother gesture.

I walk along the corridor and through the locker room and the arched door to watch the cars arriving, then up the stairs to the classrooms. I walk from one place to the other with a look of direction, pretending I'm on an errand. I like the sense of freedom.

The deep voices of men are changing the feeling in the corridors, and especially the laughing that bursts open the air. The nuns blush and smile around the fathers.

I walk into my own classroom. Sister Campion is there with her clipboard, showing some parents the history project, and Eliza and Pen's colourful picture of a woman on a ducking stool.

A father says, 'The drawing's rather good,' pointing to my poster, and I slip out of the door in case Sister Campion sees that I've heard the praise and makes me ashamed of being pleased.

I walk along the corridor. Today I can even walk past Mother Agatha's office and not be afraid. Agatha Bagatha. The Bag. I felt relieved when I found out she was called The Bag. I could even see it: black leather like a pouch purse with gathers and a silver clip that went 'Snip!' and, even though it was the kind that could catch a sliver of skin when you snapped it shut, the name diminished her a little.

There is a small group outside her office. Mother Agatha is standing next to one of the fathers. Perhaps he wants to take his daughter out for dinner. He suddenly slips his arm round Mother Agatha's waist and gives it a little squeeze. She is delighted and smiles an uncontrollable smile. Her gnarled old face, her moving back and forth on suddenly dainty feet, blushing, and tossing her veil a little with a flirtatious look is hard to behold. She looks down gaily at her black lace-up shoe, the toe incongruously pointing and drawing half-circles on the floor.

I have to walk past very fast and skip down the wooden stairs to get away from the disturbing sight of Mother Agatha being a little girl, sixty years too late.

I walk through the expanding crowd.

Miss Tweedie, unfamiliar without her white lab-coat, is wearing a blue-and-red-spotted dress with a large white collar and puffy sleeves. She is standing with her legs apart, talking eagerly to one of the mothers and gesticulating with enthusiasm. She looks as if she's wearing someone else's dress.

It's a relief to see the colours moving through the school, flowered prints, and pink and orange stripes. The old girls wear purple rosettes, and greet each other with clapping squeals. The mothers' jingling bracelets and wafting fragrance transform the atmosphere.

And then it happens.

I see him, tall and slim like a lily. He must be someone's brother. I have to look away.

There's a stalk down the centre of my body and something rushes up it and opens a flower in my throat. I have to look back. He is standing still.

He wears a jacket that opens like a door so I can see his shirt underneath. A rectangle of pale-blue that I want to put my hand on. I want to put my hand there, by the pocket, my whole palm, with the fingers spread out, and feel the warmth under my hand and the heart beating. It would be his heart beating under my hand.

He smiles and bows his head politely to Mother

Perpetua. He has dimples when he smiles, and I see the dimples in his cheeks and the sun breaks out inside me in great beams that light up the dimple and the cheek and the chin, that is smooth but not quite smooth, and the fringe over his eyes that he brushes away. And there is something clear and singing in the air around his head and in the square dark-blue shoulders of his jacket as he passes by, his bigger hands than mine by his sides and his slightly faded trousers.

And then he's gone down the corridor and I watch his hair, shining brown, disappear into the Upper School and his path has left a spicy trail through the air. And I walk in his footsteps, hoping to catch one of his thoughts from the left-behind space, wanting to be in the place his body was in, and that mysterious rectangle of pale-blue, through the dark-blue door of his jacket, and under the pale-blue the warm, and the beating sound of his very own heart. I want to rest my cheek there and hear it beating. And I walk through the people, but I can't follow him into the Upper School.

I sit down on the bench outside the chemistry lab, and hold my hands in a cup, and gaze into the cup at the boy.

I have sat for a little while when Sister Campion strides along the passage with her clipboard. She notices me sitting on the bench and comes over and sits down beside me. Sister Campion has two layers. The top layer is kind and warm. I try to get a glimpse of what is going on underneath. It might be something very cold.

She takes my hand, and looks at me with sympathetic eyes.

'I know it is difficult for you, that no one has come especially for you on this special day, and all the other girls have their families, and you are probably thinking it's because no one cares about you.' She squeezes my hand. 'In times like these we must offer up our disappointment to God, as a penance for our sins, and think of others, all the girls who have no parents to care for them, no home to go to.'

Yes, like Tracy. I think to myself. And I wonder how Sister Campion would take to Tracy in her T-shirt of Snow White having sex with the seven dwarfs, and I think, thank God I didn't tell Very about Function Day. And Very would have come, I'd never live it down, I'd never be allowed out again, I'd have to stay with the nuns in the holidays, like Lydia Farquharson had to.

'Yes, Sister,' I say, nodding and looking at my trapped hand.

The concert hall is dark. The windows are high up and the walls are brown. It is always chilly. I am not participating in the performance. We had to do a test with Mother Perpetua. We had to line up in the corridor outside piano room seventeen and sing the scales up and down: fa fa fa fa fa fa fa faaaaaa. I was so frightened that when I opened my mouth a little creaking sound came out. I couldn't explain it.

'Come along, dear, open your mouth, stand up straight.'

I opened my mouth and pulled my shoulders back but nothing at all came out then.

'Sorry, Sister.'

'Well, you can't be in the performance for Function Day.'

'I know, Sister. I'm better when there's other people singing.'

She shook her head, a little disgusted with me. If you couldn't sing what was the point of you.

'Well, you can stand at the side as long as you mouth the words but don't sing.'

I said I didn't mind sitting out of the performance, and she nodded, rather relieved.

So I don't have to stand up on the wooden movable stairs arranged in a semicircle at the end of the concert hall in my beige Function dress and be conducted to sing 'Greensleeves' with all my heart, which it has turned out is a very lucky thing.

I can't see his face. He is sitting at the back and I'd never have seen him from all that way down the other end. I can see the edge of his face, just the side by his ear. The dimple comes and goes. I don't want to stare, I just want to have his presence there so even if I close my eyes I can feel it, like when you look at the sun and it leaves a splash of turquoise on your eyeball, outlined in pink, that changes colour for a long time after. So I close my eyes and feel him there, his presence burning its shape on to my inner eye, and the singing can last for ever for all I care.

*　　*　　*

'What's up, Olive?'

She has her face pressed up to the window, trying to see into the darkness. Her sigh has misted up the glass. She rubs it away to get a better look, and shields her eyes from the light.

The supper queue is crawling along. Lower Four are pale and tear-stained. They've had to say goodbye to their parents. The prefects are sullen. The Upper School are allowed out for supper, but not prefects.

Olive comes away from the window and sighs again. 'What is it?'

'The Geminid shower,' she says. 'A perfect night. Can't see it.' She goes back to the window.

Natalie and the games captain both have sisters in Upper School, so they have gone out to supper. I am sad she isn't here. I want to tell Natalie about the boy. I saved her a place in the concert hall but the games captain gave me such a dirty look it contracted my ventricles, and I knew that you must never *ever* save a place for someone else's best friend.

Eliza is standing in front of me and keeps kicking Pen's ankles.

'Stop it!' whines Pen, and kicks her back.

Just then a tall prefect with black hair and big shoulders comes out of the refectory door.

She strides up to Eliza, leans up close, puts one arm round her neck, and whispers, 'Tell-tale tit, your tongue will be split, and all the little slugs and worms'll have a little bit!'

She catches hold of Eliza's nipple through her cardigan and pinches it and twists, so Eliza opens her mouth wide in pain but no sound comes out.

The girl stomps off, her pleated skirt swinging from side to side. Eliza has turned towards the wall but she does not sob or cry. She rubs her breast under her cardigan with tears splashing out of her eyes and keeps quiet. My mouth is wide open and I watch as my hand involuntarily rises to cover it.

I look round to see if anyone else saw.

'Shsh,' says Hen.

'But what did she tell?'

'She didn't. It's in case she does.' Hen whispers.

'Then why doesn't she?'

'You must be joking! Imelda's her sister. They share a room at home.'

'What are you looking at, NEW girl,' Eliza says through her teeth, although I am not looking at her.

'Nothing,' I stammer. 'The Geminid shower,' I say, and join Olive peering into the indigo night and the bright stars flickering over the dark trees.

Outside the chapel the double doors swing back and forth as the nuns come and go from the convent to the school, exchanging the smells of musty books for toast and porridge. In the air around their long black habits, and the wind that travels in the veils when they walk fast down the long stone corridors, are untold stories that come alive in my mind and play themselves in pictures before my eyes. I don't want them, and I don't know why there are so many, because the nuns don't want them, or don't know they are there. Even the terrible stories of the virgin martyrs, and Christ dying for our sins, even the rocks in their backs, with the doors on top, and the nails driven into bare flesh, with all the details that make Sister Clitherow's white face glow with moisture, are not as terrible as the feelings that break open inside you when you walk into one of those untold stories that hang in the air around the nuns' veils.

'What do I mean by the flesh?'

'I know it!' says Piggy.

'I'm testing Jenny, not you. Shut up.'

'By the flesh I mean my own corrupt . . . something and passions,' says Jenny.

Remove are practising for Mother Agatha. Catechisms are flying up and down the breakfast queue.

'Come on, what and passions?'

Our half has Miss Tweedie's biology test, but I'm not worried about digestion.

'The tubular passage extending from the mouth to the anus . . .' says Hen.

'I didn't ask alimentary canal, you anus, I asked peristalsis,' says Piggy.

The queue reaches the letter bench. Still Very's letter hasn't arrived. Knowing her, she's stuffed it in the back of her sketch book and forgotten to post it.

'The succession of waves of involuntary muscular contraction of various bodily tubes, especially of the alimentary tract, where it effects transport of food and waste products . . .'

I look out the window. The trees are billowing and breathing the wind. Leaves fly off in gusts and the rain is hitting the panes.

Very said London was a monster that breathed yellow and black smoke. And when we walked down the stairs into the dark tunnels she said we'd got swallowed by it.

'Today we're in the belly of the city, sliding through its guts and along its complicated small intestines,' she said when we were rattling along in the noisy tube.

'What are we now then?' I'd asked when we emerged on to the pavement at Embankment.

'Biggies!' she'd said, and we both cracked up because she'd said it too loud, and people looked round.

We'd walked out into the twilight. The clouds were pink and the buildings were cut in half. Below in blue shadow the high-storey windows lit up pink, reflecting the setting sun. We'd walked along the river looking at the pink light. Very said what was the point of being swallowed by the monster when you could see the starlings flying under the bridge in a crowd that moved with breathtaking precision like a piece of silk floating to the ground.

'OK, OK, *inclinations* and passions . . .'

'Which are . . .'

'Which are . . . shit, I always forget this bit.'

We'd taken it in turns to carry the rolled-up canvas and the stretchers because they were so bulky and kept bumping into people. It was for her interior of Big

Terry's club that'll never be paid for now. She told me what she would paint and asked my advice.

'By the flesh I mean my own corrupt inclinations and passions which are the greatest of all my enemies.'

'Is Catherine Ellis in this queue?' says an Upper Five, coming round the corner.

Everyone looks at me.

'Yes,' I say.

'Mother Agatha wants to see you.'

My heart drops into my stomach. My stomach slides into my throat.

'Now?' I ask, in a voice far too high.

The Upper Five nods.

'What's it for?' asks Piggy.

The Upper Five shrugs.

'Have you been smoking, Cath?'

'She will be soon.'

And I follow the Upper Five down the corridor, to Mother Agatha's office door.

The light is red. I knock. The light stays red. She always makes you wait. They've found out about Granny. It must be that. I'm so scared my eyes won't shut. I try to imagine Very in her wellingtons, her stripy jersey with the holes in the elbows and that long flowing skirt that she tried to iron while she had it on, and I wonder what *she* would say to Mother Agatha when she curled her hands like claws and looked at you through black eyes with the whites showing along the bottom lids. I don't think Very would be frightened. She belongs to another world. She has to worry about the man downstairs, and Big Terry, and Mrs McGonogall's long yellow arms. She has to worry about the dark streets, and men with skinheads, and tattoos of skulls under their ear lobes. She has to worry about gangs of white-faced, black-haired girls who might spit at you in a nightclub and trying to find a job, and not panicking when the woman with dyed hair says 'Stupid fuckin' bitch', or the red-faced butcher with popping-out eyes touches her bosom when he put sawdust in the breast pocket of her shirt. He even asked her to go down into the cellar where there was lots of sawdust and she could fill a shoebox, but she said no, the rats didn't need that much.

The light turns green.

There are patterns in front of my eyes.

I turn the handle and walk in. I am breathing fast and I have a strange sensation of a stone room with bolted doors. She sits at her desk. The light in the room looks black. I am breathing knives and the air is hot, like hot metal. There is a man behind her, standing with his hands behind his back. But then he isn't there. She doesn't look up. She is writing. You have to do that, stand there breathing, seeing men who aren't there, swallowing hot metal until she's finished writing.

But then I see it. The envelope. With Very's writing on the front. Addressed to me. It is open. The letter is unfolded. My letter. And there are jagged lines all around the room. Switching and flicking, and something red is rising in my chest.

'Sit down, dear.'

But I can't take my eyes off the letter. I am swallowing.

My heart is beating fast. I can't breathe. I want to scream, 'That's my letter! What are you doing with my sister's letter!' But I'm afraid, and the fear slithers through me.

I feel hot and angry and afraid. And still she keeps on writing. She must know I can see the letter.

'Sit down, my child,' she says, and points to the chair. I look at her face, and at the letter, and at her face. She nods to the chair.

I wobble backwards and sit down.

'Your sister's name is Verity, isn't it, dear?'

She picks up the letter.

I don't want to see Very's writing in her shiny fingers.

'Yes, Mother.'

'THIS' – she is holding it between her thumb and forefinger – 'is from Verity, is it? VERY is Verity, is that right?'

'Very's my sister,' I say.

She folds the letter up slowly and puts it into the envelope. She takes her glasses off, swallows, and puts them in her glasses case. She clears her throat with her teeth clenched together so I can see the muscles of her jaw bulge out.

'Well,' she says, looking at me, 'we don't think it is appropriate for you to stay with your sister again and we have outlined as much in a letter to your parents. We cannot forbid you from writing to your sister, but we can suggest to your parents that she is not an appropriate influence.' She puts her glasses back on, opens the book she was writing in before, looks down, and says, 'You may go.'

I stand up, 'But Mother . . .'

She continues writing.

'My letter.'

I reach out my hand to take the letter. Without looking up she grabs it quickly and puts it slowly in her drawer.

'We will say no more about the letter. You may go.'

As I open the door, without raising her head or ceasing to write, she says, 'One rotten apple rots the barrel,' and I close the door.

I walk up the stairs outside the office and along the bathroom corridor. Yellow D is out of bounds. I sit in the dark-blue bathroom and look out on the corner of the tiled roof. It is wet with rain and water is sliding down the inner corner and filling up the gutters. Very's letter. I keep clasping and unclasping my hands. I see it folded up and shut in the dark. I can smell the musty drawer. Where will Mother Agatha put it in the end? It is my letter, those are my words, from my Very. What did you write, Very? What was it? Not that quote about the monstrous eggs hatching that you told me by the green water. Oh Very, not that!

The bell rings. I walk down the stairs with heavy legs, and into the classroom. Only a few minutes till history.

'What happened, Cath?'

'What did The Bag want?'

Girls gather round my desk.

All I can say in a cracked voice is, 'My sister's letter. She's got my sister's letter.'

Piggy pats my back and Hen offers me a hanky and Lucy hands me, nodding, 'Yes, you can, take it!,' the remains of her sherbert dip-dab, and the door opens and Sister Scholastica walks in.

I blow my nose behind my desk-lid and pull out my history textbook and Sister Scholastica begins to read. I think of her cupboard full of exercise books and the smell of paper and new pencils. Her monotonous voice is soothing and the rain beats against the window like tiny nails. I see soldiers riding across the fields in grey steel helmets. The metal makes a clanking sound and the hooves thud across the plough. It is autumn and the sun is low. I'm trying to see where they are going but it just fades into a blue mist.

'The Battle of Edgehill? Thank you, Natalie.'

'Commander of the Parliamentary Army?'

'Earl of Essex, Sister.'

Then I am in a grey-stone town square. Down one side the buildings are built of wood with black beams. There are chickens running across the mud and cobbles and horses clinking, a crowd of mud-spattered people, their faces grimy, talking, some laughing, a woman with grey hair holding a basket with a white goose in it. It is tied in, its long neck stretches and opens its mouth, I can see its orange tongue.

'Henrietta can you tell me his name?'

'Oliver Cromwell, Sister.'

'Well done, dear. And what are his dates? Please . . . anybody? Yes, Penelope, dear?'

Suddenly the air is filled with the smell of smoke,

sweet-smelling. A horse in harness throws its head back, curls its lips and neighs loudly. The nostrils quiver, the crowd murmurs. Through the people, children clutching the muddy skirts of women, is a clearing. In the clearing is a stack of wood that has just been lit. The faggots are tied together with rope that is smoking and beginning to catch light, the sweet smell, a soft rain hisses on the flames.

Then I see them, a girl and an old woman. The girl is not much older than me, the woman could be her grandmother. They are in the centre, trussed up together against a tall stick. The old woman holds the girl's hand, whose eyes are wide open with terror, every part of her body trembling, whimpering, the old woman, her stare almost vacant, clutching at the girl's hand. Suddenly the girl screams, a guttural terrified scream that tears your heart, the crowd shifts, the horses neigh from every corner of the square as though answering. Her head drops forward, she has fainted.

'No, dear, it's the seventeenth century. James I came to the throne in 1601. Does anyone know the name of Charles I's son?'

'Charles II.'

'Well done, dear.'

The bell rings. Sister Scholastica closes her book.

'Thank you, girls.'

We stand up and say, 'Thank you, Sister Scholastica.'

She sweeps out of the room, her thin black veil floating in the air behind her.

*   *   *

I am sitting huddled up on a plastic window seat in the porch of the Middle School library with the rain falling outside in vertical torrents. The girl's cry is ringing in me. It scooped out a hollow place that makes the sounds echo. Tonight we are going into retreat. Three days of silence that start with supper.

The rain drums on to the fibre-glass roof so the vibration fills me as I watch it overflow the gullies and run over the lawn in brown streams. Water is gushing down the drainpipes and digging muddy holes in the grass. I want to stand outside naked in the torrent so the drops fall through me, in between the spinning atoms, wash right through me. I want to be made of rain.

'What are you doing down here during lunch? You know you're not allowed!' It's Sister Felicity, without her smile.

'Oh Sister, I'm sorry. I didn't know we weren't allowed,' I say, standing up too quickly, so Sister Felicity disappears behind a curtain of exploding fireworks and I have to hold on to the wooden shelf to stop myself falling over.

'You knew very well. That's two conduct marks!' And she gets out her little red book. 'Upstairs, please, and I will confiscate the book.'

I give her the book I haven't opened.

'But I really didn't know I wasn't allowed. Sister,' I say.

'You knew perfectly well,' she says, and snaps the book under her arm and drops the red book into a pocket in her habit.

'Upstairs at once.' She points upwards and I hobble away on my pins-and-needles legs.

I ask Piggy when I get upstairs, 'Is the Middle School library out of bounds at lunchtime?'

'Yes, of course,' she says. 'Everybody knows that.'

After lunch I'm on washing up. Pen has a clarinet lesson at the end of study and she said she'd get me a good place in the phone queue if I did her shift. I have to speak to Very before the retreat silence begins. The dish-washing machines make loud whooshing sounds and clunks. Piggy is on duty as well and we look at each other in our blue plastic caps, like bath caps, and plastic aprons and yellow rubber gloves up to our elbows. We have to wear our wellies in the back kitchens because there is water all over the red tiles.

We scrape the piles of dirty plates and stack them in the blue plastic boxes with holes in, and send them though the split see-through curtain, where they clink and tremble through on the conveyor belt. The noise of the machines is so loud you have to shout and even then it's hard to hear. When we have finished stacking them in one end we have to walk carefully past the shining metal machine without touching it because it is very hot and it chugs and shakes and steam pours out of it so the air is moist and we collect a film of wet on our faces and aprons. We mop the floor while we wait for the machines.

We can hear the swirl and swoosh of the water and then after a shrill choking sound a whoosh of steaming bubbly water comes gushing out of a black tube and into a drain. The machine chugs and coughs again and the plates and cups and glasses and spoons and knives and forks begin to shake and rattle their way under the yellow split curtain at the other end. They are boiling hot and we have to pull out the trays and stack them up on to the side fast so they don't bump into one another. We wipe the plates quickly – they are so hot they dry themselves, and stack them back in the trolleys, sorting the spoons and knives and forks and stacking them alongside in net containers.

But when I reach the phone box the queue is seven girls long, and there is no sign of Pen.

I think she must have forgotten until Eliza walks past with a smirky look on her face and says, 'Still waiting?' and I hear them snorting and giggling round the corner.

Father Vincent is the retreat priest. He is thin, with a pale face and unreachable eyes. He keeps taking out his handkerchief to wipe his mouth. I can tell he doesn't like getting dirty because the board pen he used to write 'SIN' on the flip chirt has got on to his fingers and he keeps looking down at his fingers and frowning then trying to wipe away the ink with his handkerchief, but it's indelible marker and it doesn't come off. Even though he knows it doesn't come off he keeps looking at it with a worried face.

I stood in the telephone queue for an hour and a half last night. When it was finally my turn the phone in

Very's flat just rang and rang. I let it ring for my whole fifteen minutes, pretending to talk and laugh so they wouldn't knock on the window, all the time saying, 'Very, please answer, please answer. What will I do if I can't stay with you?'

The rain is still lashing the panes. Father Vincent looks up, frowns at the girls all sitting around the tables in the Middle School common room with our catechisms and missals and new notebooks called retreat notebooks which you must treat with especial respect though you're allowed to paste a holy card on the front. 'It's not a rough book, so no doodling.' We are waiting for him to start speaking. We have read the word 'SIN'.

But he stands there frowning at the girls and frowning at the black ink on his fingers and tries again to wipe it off.

He turns around to the flip chart and, after underlining 'SIN', he writes 'ORIGINAL' and 'ACTUAL' underneath. Then he subdivides 'ACTUAL' into 'MORTAL' and 'VENIAL'.

He turns around once more and takes out his handkerchief to wipe his mouth, looks down at his dirty fingers, tries to wipe away the ink again, looks up and frowns at us.

He clears his throat and begins to speak in a high voice. It is hard to hear him over the rain.

'We will begin with original sin, our hereditary sinfulness.' He turns to the chart, points to the words, and clears his throat. 'All mankind has contracted the guilt and stain of original sin.'

His voice stays on the same note, as though he is

pointing out the periodic table, not this terrible news. I
see the stain spreading through me, like black ink. We
have inherited this guilt from Adam, the head of all
mankind, who committed the sin of disobedience when
he ate the forbidden fruit. But it was Eve, the first sinner,
who tempted Adam.

'We ourselves commit ACTUAL sin,' he continues,
pointing to the word. 'There are two kinds of ACTUAL
sin, MORTAL and VENIAL. Mortal sin kills the soul
and deserves hell.'

I start worrying about Very and if she has killed her
soul.

'It is the greatest of all evils to fall into mortal sin, and
they who die in mortal sin will go to hell for all eternity.'

I try to remember if fornication counts as mortal, and
break into a cold sweat.

'. . . because the wicked also shall live for ever and be
punished in the fires of hell.'

And I imagine her in her vest and pants with orange
flames licking her long white legs, her hair catching alight,
and her face looking the way it did when she shut her
thumb in the door, before she said 'OW' then 'FUCK'.

It makes my palms sweat and my heart beat fast and a
horrible sick feeling rise up from my stomach to my
throat but when it reaches my throat it is heavy and feels
like crying, and I want to get up and kick at Father
Vincent's legs, and get his black pen and scribble all over
his neat letters and screw up the paper and stuff it into
his little wet mouth so he can't tell me any more about
sin and Very and hell.

He turns again to the flip chart and draws a diagram which indicates levels of sin, heaven, hell and purgatory. And I look gloomily at the floor as everyone copies down the subdivisions and think, what's the point of being in heaven if Very's not there? And I'll have to sit with Mother Agatha and Father Vincent with God down at the other end in a seating arrangement with Jesus, while everyone I met in London is in hell with Very. Eddie, Big Terry, Tracy, even the man we met waiting for the bus. He said it was the most exciting thing he'd ever done, and that's not repentance.

When we've done SIN, Original, Actual, Mortal and Venial, we go on to atonement. God sent his son to die on earth, to atone for Adam's sin, and every sin we commit is like hammering a nail into Jesus's bare hands. We go through all the agonies of Jesus, being lashed, mocked, crowned with thorns, nailed up and hanging there by the nails, then pierced with the spear. It is a horrible slow death. And 'those who sin grievously have wilfully crucified the Son of God and openly mocked him.'

I wonder if he knew that, the man at the bus stop. Very asked him if he'd killed anyone, but he didn't answer that question, he just kept saying, 'Most exciting thing I ever did.'

Father Vincent is flipping the flip chart to find a clean page, and writes 'CONTRITION' at the top.

It was cold that night and I had my hand in Very's warm pocket along with her hand because we were sharing the gloves. We tried clapping, but we managed twiddling our thumbs quite well. That's why we were laughing. There was frost on the cars that night – you could even see the stars above the street lights.

He'd stood really close to us holding a can of Tennant's Superlager under his chin, and joined in the laughing. He said it was the most exciting thing he'd ever done and even though he was slurring his words Very's always interested in things like that. She said, 'Did you? How many were you? Did you get the money?' They were all in the back, he said, looking out the peep hole, and one of the lads said, 'You know this is illegal,' and they'd all laughed.

Father Vincent points to the prayer he has just written on to the flip chart and we open our mouths and call on God to beg pardon for our sins and tell him we detest them above all things, that they deserve his dreadful punishments because they have crucified our loving saviour, and because they offend God's infinite goodness.

He got fifteen years but only did ten.

'You didn't kill anyone, did you?' Very asked.

I don't think he did but anyway he didn't answer. He just kept saying, 'Most exciting thing I ever did,' and nodding at his can of lager. 'Armed robbery, they called it!' And then he looked at both of us. 'I never knew him, though.' His head was wobbling a bit. 'It just said "Fisherman from Aberdeen" on the birth certificate. "Fisherman from Aberdeen."' He wrote it in the air, then underlined it. 'I'd like to have, seen him, you know, not to speak to, just seen him, pointed, that's him!' And he put his index finger in front of his eyes and did a wobbling point. 'That's him, that's my father.'

Then the bus came and when I looked back at him he was on the pavement still mouthing 'That's him' and trying to get his finger to point straight.

We walk in single file. The retreat silence has grown heavy. Lucy has to walk at the back with Sister Campion so she doesn't misbehave. She has been told off with silent, cutting eyes. Lucy makes faces at everyone whenever she gets the chance, rolling her eyes and wiping her brow to indicate 'How long will this last?' mimicking dying people in imitation agonies.

At breakfast in the big deserted refectory she had to sit at a long refectory table on her own, because she did the elephant trick with a glass of milk, then got the giggles with her mouth full, and sprayed porridge all over the floor. She had to sit there on her own with her back to us.

Piggy gets them too, but she has perfected the art of laughing behind her crossed arms. She manages to keep the giggles in her stomach. She has a serious look on her face but her eyes are glassy. You would hardly know unless you were sitting beside her and could feel the vibration of it.

We file into the refectory and Lucy is allowed to sit with the rest of us for lunch. We scrape the chairs back and all the noises are loud. The clattering knives and forks, the sounds of chewing and swallowing. The games captain has a click in her jaw. People glare at it as though giving it a dirty look will stop it clicking. But we daren't catch each other's eye in case it sets us off.

You have to look down at your food, at the shiny brown gravy and the stringy meat. At the peas mixed with cubes of carrot, sweetcorn and green beans, and the runny mashed potato, for-mash-get-Smash. Lucy has red eyes and is finding it hard to swallow. She looks at the curtain rail, trying to chew, with her eyes full of tears. She's been told off once too often.

We take our trays through to the pantry and unload them into the still-empty baskets and follow Sister Campion along the corridor and down the stairs to the locker room.

'Wellingtons' was written on the flip chart in the common room. Sister Campion stands by watching us as we pull on our brown macs and wellies. There was frost on the roof of the gym when I looked out the window of Yellow D. After all that rain there will be ice.

I remember screaming in a dream and waking up with a thin wail and a terrified jolt. I opened the curtain to see the just-before-dawn sky and watch the sliver of light, breathing and sweating and clutching on to the bit of windowsill on my side of the partition. The roof of the gym was white with frost.

But when I walk out into the light the air has warmed, and the frost has melted. We are supposed to be thinking about God. But most of us are thinking about Mother Agatha's talk on the Doctrine of the Catholic Faith which is really a catechism test, that is going to happen directly after our walk.

The day is thawing, but frost is on the cold side of the banks. We are allowed to bring prayer books to read, the way the novices do, in their short veils and knee-length grey skirts, walking under the trees with their heads bowed, or the postulants who still wear home clothes but always look drab. So we walk through the spitting rain under the trees in our brown macs with catechism booklets hidden in our prayer books.

I have worried so much about the holidays and Very that I can't worry any more. But when I think of Mother Agatha's talk on the Doctrine of the Catholic Faith, of her eyes looking at me and seeing the rotten apple, my toes curl up and my feet turn sideways inside my wellingtons. A mesh of tiny threads under my skin lights up with dread, and as the time approaches the feeling intensifies.

The air smells of mud, and there is the sound of a small rain river rushing and gurgling in the wood. I look down at the brown mud and the leaves in the mud, and the grass and the feathers in the mud, and the stones. I can't look up. I watch the texture stiff and slithery and the twiggy plants reflected in the puddles. I slide in and make sucking footsteps and swish through the muddy water.

I can't look at the sky, my head is bowed. All of me is turned inward. I am afraid of seeing the rotten apple. If it is really there. I have no defence against her eyes. The puddles are deep, I slide through the puddles. Light rain touches my skin. There is invisible ice, just below the water surface, that cracks. Under the ice are bubbles which make swirling patterns with white lines.

Mud and ice and puddles of water. But I can't look up. It cracks and splits like panes of glass and slides above the brown water. Nuns always look down. So they never see the sky.

I come to the roots of a tree, clutching into the mud and the black stones. I stand next to the tree. A crow calls from a field. The roots are covered in moss but the trunk is smooth and grey. The bright-green moss is soaking up the rain. It looks like a big green hand, spread out, soft velvet moss covering every finger. In between the fingers, furry grass is growing sideways trapping the discarded orange leaves.

Suddenly the tree speaks like a clear note above a noise.

'I'm here,' it says.

We sit in a nervous audience waiting for Mother Agatha. There are sounds of breathing, and the clock ticking. Sometimes someone clears her throat, or rearranges her skirt.

My plan went wrong. After we'd arranged the chairs into rows, I was lingering at the far end of the room, ready to grab a seat at the back, when Sister Campion noticed 'Wellingtons' on the flip chart. She motioned to me to turn over to a clean page. I had to walk across the room, as everyone was sitting down, and turn the page of the flip chart.

If only I hadn't looked round at the exact moment Sister

Campion saw 'Wellingtons'. If only I'd been looking the other way, she wouldn't have pointed at me, and at the flip chart, and nodded, and I wouldn't be sitting here in the middle of the front row, right under Mother Agatha's nose.

The feeling in the common room becomes tense. We can hear Mother Agatha walking along the corridor. Soon she will arrive. The door with small leaded panes opens. She sweeps through in her tight-laced black shoes. I sit between Natalie and Piggy. We are holding our breath. We can feel the wind from her veil in our faces. She walks up and down on crêpe soles that squeak on the wooden floor, and surveys us slowly, one by one. The force in her eyes is like a magnet and her presence thickens the air.

She holds her hands in fists. Her face is mottled.

'Henrietta Whitehouse, WHY must we love God?'

Hen stands up. She is short for twelve, her horse-thick hair in a hairband. She clears her throat and blushes all the way down her neck.

'We must love God because he is infinitely good in himself, and he is infinitely good to us.' Hen sits down again and all her muscles relax, I can see her melting on to the chair. It has finished – she will not be chosen twice.

Mother Agatha walks up and down again, like an animal waiting to strike. I sit on the edge of my chair in case she pounces on me.

'Jenny, does God know and see all things?'

Jenny stands up, a pale lanky girl, and answers in a high voice.

'God knows and sees all things, even our most secret thoughts.'

I'm suddenly terrified by this, as though Mother Agatha's black eyes can see right into my mind, that it is not private, that everything is there for her to see and disapprove of, and through my eyes she can see all Very's sins too. I want to say I am not like Very, I am good. Just because she's my sister. I am not like her.

'Penelope Shuttleworth, what must you do to save your soul?'

Pen stands up. She has freckles and a crack in her voice.

'To save my soul I must love God with faith, hope and charity . . .'

Everyone waits and looks from Mother Agatha to Pen as she stands with her mouth open, looking desperately out the window to remember what else she must do to save her soul. '. . . and love him with my whole heart.'

Everyone breathes a sigh of relief that she has re-membered. And I see a picture of my whole heart in my mind and I know that it doesn't love God, that it doesn't even like him, and Mother Agatha can see, and that's why she thinks I will rot the barrel.

Mother Agatha strides up and down. She stops, she turns round to face us.

'Luke 9.23. "If any man will come after me, let him deny himself, and take up his cross daily . . ."' She writes Luke 9.23 on the flip chart.

'HOW are we to deny ourselves?' she bellows. 'We are to deny ourselves by GIVING UP our own will, and by GOING AGAINST our own humours, inclinations and passions.'

We all quiver inside trying to locate our inclinations

and passions so we can work out how to go against them. I know that Mother Agatha has done it – the iron force in her has crushed them. Her humour and passion are no more, and she has done it right. There is not one chink of doubt.

She walks across the room and stops. Even before she reaches me I can feel her presence like a dark wind move towards me through the air. She is at the other end of the room but she has picked me out. Though I can't see it, I know that through the window behind my head you can see into the wood, and there is a tree there, with mossy roots . . .

'Stand up, Catherine Ellis.'

. . . and a rain-river runs over the wet leaves to the marsh, where it spreads out reflecting the sky. I stand up. . . . and behind the trees is a river, a secret red river, and if you press your palms over your ears, even in study, you can hear it rushing.

'Why are we bound to deny ourselves?'

. . . and there is a cave there, because I found it behind the brambles and the bindweed, and you can walk right into the cave that smells of wet earth, and hear the sound of the river in your ears.

'We are bound to deny ourselves . . .' and through the echoes of water and the rippling light on the wall is a quietness, and behind the quietness is the sound talking to you from your own bones. 'Because . . . because . . . our natural inclinations . . .'

But I can't remember it. I stand in the huge silence and swallow, and the room fills with panic and loud noises inside my ears.

Mother Agatha looks at me, and under her gaze I turn into a rotten apple, small and contagious. I want to shout, 'I am not like Very, she just wrote that letter, but I'm not like her. I don't even like her really, she's just my sister, it's not my fault, she might be rotten but I'm not.'

But Mother Agatha looks at me with her magnetic eyes. She walks too near to me and hands me the catechism book opened at the right page. She motions for me to stand in front of the lined-up chairs. I squeak across the wooden floor and she nods for me to read.

'I am bound to deny myself,' my voice is small and quavery in the big room, 'because my nature from my very childhood is prone to evil.' I look up, drawn by her watching, and something slithers out of her eyes and into mine. She nods for me to continue.

'. . . and if not corrected by self-denial will certainly carry me to hell.'

I look at her and wait for her to nod for me to sit down. She nods. I sit down.

It is over.

I don't even notice putting the chairs back into place. I have gone into a kind of trance, and in the hours of contemplation before lunch I find the slithering thing has a presence inside me. It talks, and tells me of my nature prone to evil, and my besmirched soul:

You just want to do the history project so you can show off you're good at drawing.

You only gave Hen your green pen because you want her to like you. You are bad, that's why, born bad.

You're false – you suck up to people and want them to like you because you're trying to hide how bad you are.

You're a coward. You didn't stand up for Olive when Teddy was bitching, because you're weak.

You even disown Very, your own sister.

And I know that it is true.

I feel as if I'm locked in a small room, with walls of red stone. I am clenched with shame. I writhe in the pain of being bad. Far away there is a piercing sadness.

Before long, things are turning back to front and altering their shape – they make new sense inside me. Very is bad, Mother Agatha cares about my soul, suffering is holy, my nature is evil, self-denial is good.

Natalie and I deny ourselves quiche and potatoes and have bread without butter at lunch. Saint John of the Cross says, 'Let your soul turn always not to what tastes best but to what is most distasteful,' so we have the pea soup.

And all afternoon it is silent thought, but you can read prayer books, and Saint John of the Cross says, 'Despise yourself and wish that others should despise you,' and I suppose it means that then you'll become good. And in the silence and the long afternoon hours in the common room with the wind rattling the small leaded panes the voice gets louder and more insistent, and if I listen maybe I will become good.

When I walk down the stairs to Mass, everything has gone blank. Only the voice is awake. Telling me I'm wrong, not good enough, informing me of my stain.

I stand in chapel on the edge of my feet. My threads don't join up. All the hairs on my head are holding on to my scalp and I am filled with a kind of dampness. Something in me is crying with a faraway sound.

The air in the chapel is thick with what we must not do and should not be. My hands seem unfamiliar. We kneel down and bend over and put our faces between our fingers and the great weight of the air comes to rest on our shoulders. ' "Lord, I am not worthy to receive you," ' and I hear people cracking apart and then the sound disappears and I hear rushing. I feel suffocated by the weight of the air. I am falling forward listening to the thread of light, a clear voice singing the Agnus Dei.

The chapel ceiling turns very slowly upside down. I feel a thud, and the high notes mix with the streak of sunlight shining through the diamond-shaped pane in the roof, and I wonder how it is I am up here escaping out through the opening the sun has entered in, gliding through the outside air. I see myself by the forbidden river, but transparent, and in the elongated moment before everything turns black I hear the river singing through the ears of my see-through self.

*　　*　　*

'Do we have you back now then?' It is a Welsh voice.

I half open my eyes.

'Ah we do, I think we do.'

I see her blurred face come close up to mine, and smell her lavender breath.

'Are you here with us at last?'

I shake my head carefully.

'No?'

She gets up and opens the window a crack. I am surprised to see it is light outside. She is very small.

I close my eyes. There is an ache in the air and I don't know if it is mine or belongs to the marsh and the flooded grass, or the gloomy sky and the moaning wind.

'So where are you then?' she says from the window.

'By the river, Sister,' I say in a husky voice.

She puts her hand over my brow and gets out her watch as though she is timing my forehead.

'No, darlin',' she says. 'You're in the infirmary. I'm Sister Dewi, and it's Thursday.'

But the moss is soaking up the rain. I can hear the river behind the wind.

My voice cracks and I say, 'No, Sister, I'm by the river,' and a tear rolls out the side of my eye and into my ear.

'There now, there now,' she says and pats my hand. 'It's all right, and what are you doin' down there, I wonder?'

'I don't even like God, Sister!' I say, suddenly terrified, and sit up.

'There now, there now,' she says, and pats my hand again. 'That's not God.'

'Who is it then?'

'Well, I'm not sure that I know that. No, I don't really know, but it's not God.'

'Are you sure?'

'I am.'

'How?'

'Because God doesn't frighten a young girl out of her wits and there it is.'

I want her to go on talking in her voice like a musical instrument, but she straightens the sheet, pats my hand, says, 'There now,' and leaves the room.

The infirmary is up in the roof and the ceiling is slanted. I lie in my bed and look out the window at the sky. It begins to rain and the drops hit the window and drip down the pane. The sky darkens and the rain turns to hail. It spatters against the glass in gusts.

Through the sound of the wind and the hail I hear footsteps walking down the corridor from far away. They get nearer and nearer and stop. There's a knock on the door. It opens before I've said, 'Come in,' and Sister Campion enters. It seems as if she is huge and fills the whole room, but maybe it's because I'm lying down.

She says, 'May I?' and sits down on the edge of the bed before I've said yes.

She picks up one of my hands and put it between hers. She keeps squashing it in a concerned way. She looks at me with her head on one side. She looks at my forehead and then at my eyes and back at my forehead like they do in old black-and-white films when he says, 'Are you happy, darling?' and she says, 'Yes, so very very happy,' and looks from his forehead to his eyes and back. It means you really love someone and can't keep your eyes off their forehead. Very and I used to practise it in the bath.

'How is our patient?' she says, but I don't want her to say 'our', I don't want to belong to her or whoever the other person is. 'You're looking better but still a little pale.'

She looks at me and nods. Then puts her hand into one of those huge hidden pockets in her black habit and pulls out the little red book with the white cross on it.

'I've brought your catechisms, dear, so you won't feel left behind,' and she's marked the page with a slip of paper. She puts the little book on the bed. 'Is everything all right, dear?'

And I nearly say something. I open my mouth and my voice is nearly making a word, drawn out by the concern in her eyes. But I keep quiet.

'Your class asked me to send you their best wishes for a speedy recovery. The girls will be offering up prayers this morning in chapel.'

'Thank you, Sister.'

When I hear her footsteps die away and I listen for a few minutes to the creaking silence under the hailstones and I'm sure she isn't coming back, I pick up the little red book with the white cross on the cover and throw it at the door.

'I don't know who you are but you're not God!' I say and wait for something terrible to happen.

But nothing does.

Only a shower of hailstones rattles down the chimney and I watch the fireplace with my heart beating as though someone is going to pop out of it like Father Christmas. But only the hailstones bounce into the hearth. Like they do in London at Very's. That's not God talking, it's just hail. It bounces through that gap between the gas fire and the fireplace on to the blue carpet. That blue carpet is covered in fluff. It needs a good hoover but Very hasn't worked out how to change the hoover bag.

I breathe out a long breath. Very made that gap when she prised the heater away from the fireplace to rescue the trapped pigeon.

She said, 'Roo-coo-coo,' and called it 'my honey bird'.

It must be windy, high up in the sky, because the clouds are moving quickly. Gradually the hail stops.

She was in a bad mood when she rang the gas man.

I only heard her shout, 'MONDAY! It'll be DEAD by Monday!' then I went to listen at the receiver.

The gas man said, 'Turn the heater on, luv, kill it quickly! They're murder when they've been shut in like that – flap about the room, cover the place in soot . . .'

We could hear it fluttering in the chimney behind the gas fire. That's when Very slammed the phone down.

'I'm not fucking killing it quickly!'

But the fluttering stopped when she prised the heater away, and put her outstretched finger through the gap. She cooed to it in roo-coo pigeon language and called it 'my dove', 'my honey bird', and it stepped calmly on to her finger through the gap, its wings bunched together black with coaldust.

And when she sat with it there, kneeling on one knee and getting up slowly, slowly, it didn't flap, it just blinked and wobbled on her finger, its red claws digging in to keep steady. So she took it to the open window and put her hand outside. Even then it just sat there. It was only when she bounced her finger up and down saying, 'Go on, go on, you're free,' that it took off and flew in a wide arc over the trees.

The dark corridor squeaks and creaks as I walk along it. I can still hear the wind up here in the roof. I want to take my rolled-up nightie and my toothbrush back to Yellow D, without bumping into Ethelbug. I hear footsteps down the corridor and a door opening. But it's only Sister Ruth in the laundry room. She smiles as I pass the open door where she stands among the ironed and unironed clothes. She has a long square face and thick black eyebrows.

'Hello, Sister.'

Her smile broadens. She is arranging our bundles, folding clothes and piling them neatly in the right pile.

'Not ready yet, dear.'

'Oh I'm not collecting my bundle, Sister – I fainted in chapel.'

She puts down the clothes and claps her hands.

'Did you now! Well done, and now you're better, well done.'

'Thank you, Sister.'

She is very pale. I think it's because she's shut in the laundry room for days on end, folding clothes, matching the nametag to the number on the shelf.

The school seems quiet and deserted. The Upper School are doing exams. I have to go down a staircase and up another one to reach Yellow D.

The long room with rows of yellow curtains and the yellow strip of carpet down the centre smells of soap and onions, except Natalie's cubicle next to mine, that smells of lily-of-the-valley talcum powder.

'I've told you before, Catherine Ellis.'

I jump. Gobby is standing behind me. She gives me a dark-red look.

'I fainted in chapel, Sister. I was in the infirmary.'

She is taken aback. Then she smiles and I see her teeth for the first time.

'Well, that's different. That's all right then, dear.'

They are absolutely regular, like little pearls. I am astonished by the beauty of her teeth.

I walk down the stairs with hesitation. I feel shy about going into the classroom and the bustle. I linger outside and listen to the voices. But when I walk through the door everyone gathers round.

'What's it like, fainting?'

'Is it true you see stars?'

'My cousin fainted once – she said it was lovely.'

And when I open my desk 'Welcome back' is sellotaped to the inside lid in eleven different colours of felt pen, and there are two Toffos on top of my retreat notebook.

'Did Sister tell you we offered up prayers?'

'Must have worked.'

'Did you get breakfast on a tray?'

I take the Toffos next door to the Remove classroom to see Olive.

She doesn't say hello, she says, 'Shall I show you how to draw three-dimensional aquariums?'

And I give her a Toffo and sit down on the other side of her desk to watch her draw them upside down.

Olive loves pi. It's pi this and pi that.

'But what *is* it, Olive?' I ask as I flick through her pink maths book.

'Three point one four one five nine is the key to the unimagined secrets of the universe,' she says, and, for a fraction of a second so small even Olive wouldn't be able to divide it, I look into the eye of the unimagined secrets of the universe and its plummeting depths make my hair stand on end so I have to rub my arms to make the goose-bumps go away.

Olive is crossing out numbers in the back of her rough book. She has calculated the hours, which take up five pages, and at the top of each column how many fewer seconds there are to go until she can go home. She misses her telescope. At any given moment she can tell you how many seconds there are left.

'How many now, Olive?'

She puts her head down and her dark hair makes a shiny curtain over her rough book.

'Three million, forty-four thousand, seven hundred and . . .' She looks at her watch. 'Twelve . . . eleven . . . ten . . .'

In the back of most rough books is a calendar crossed off every day. Below the box of numbers is usually a picture of a house with a Christmas tree in it, with 'Yippee!' or 'Freedom' written underneath. I've drawn a tiny picture of London in mine, with the river, the bridge, the tall column, and the man who shows his bronze bottom when you wind round Hyde Park Corner on the bus. Very likes the man on the plinth, showing his bottom to the passing traffic.

When we walk out of the arched door a mist has fallen. It muffles the sound of our footsteps then echoes them. We wander about breathing in the mist, waiting for the bell to ring for double art. I can't see the trees, the road is hidden, and everything is unravelling in my mind.

It started in maths. Miss Birdlip was wearing pink lipstick and Eliza said, 'Ooh what's the occasion!' because Miss Birdlip always blushes, but it didn't stop her writing up her big equation on the board and looking round after the blush had finished.

We were doing pi. Olive's favourite. Those numbers I

can't understand what they do must have unlocked the idea, because it all came out in my mind like a door opening. That's what Olive meant about pi being the key. Three point one four one five nine, and there it was, miles and miles of singing starlit space. No gnashing or chewing or spitting or burning. Just an expanse of indigo humming and bright twirling. Very won't go there because it doesn't exist. It's all safe, it's all friendly, it's all all right.

I was so relieved that I started smiling and Miss Birdlip said, 'What are you smiling for?' because she must have thought I'd been passed a note, and everyone looked round, but there was nothing to see, just a huge space in my mind where hell used to be.

'Nothing, Miss Birdlip,' I said, putting my head down and trying to frown away the smile. 'Nothing.'

The bell inside the school rings and we all troop down the path and into the art hut. Miss Sheldon looks tired. She says we can choose whatever material we like today because it's the last class and everyone cheers.

I am glad I don't have to do a linocut of a bunch of flowers and cut my finger in a V-shape with the fiddly blade, or get everything stuck together trying to plaster soaked newspaper on to a wire frame to make a pop singer who ended up looking like a frog so I painted him green when he finally dried. I pull a black dollop of shining wet clay on to the piece of hardboard, and take it to the window.

'Do wear an apron, dear, if you're working with clay.'

I put the apron over my head and sit on the high stool. The ledge runs all the way around the hut under the long windows. Behind me the gas fire whistles faintly and heats my back, but before me the glass is cool.

It's the time before dusk, the birds are quiet. The sky hasn't turned blue, but there's no more light. It must be misty on the marsh, shrouded, hushed. I knead the clay to make it soft.

I shape it into a worm and coil it into a labyrinth. I punch it and slap it and fashion a black face in the smooth surface, then roll it into a ball. I make a person and then squash her back into the clay again. I smell the wet earth and see a mauve light behind my eyes. I pat the clay flat then mould it between my fingers. It turns from a bear with claws into a crow with outspread wings.

'Very effective, dear,' says Miss Sheldon, and moves on.

Then I roll it. I roll it slowly back and forth because I am trying to remember the dream I had when I flew through the roof. I am trying to catch hold of the edge of it before it slips down behind, like a letter at the back of a drawer. I have to move slowly, hardly breathe. I see the spiral of light, feel the swift rush of air. I remember the colours flitting by like cat's eyes and a voice that blew through me like a warm wind.

I can't retrieve what I saw, but something slips into me like sunlight. I can feel the rhythm drumming in my blood. The river rushing and gulping down the bank where the sucking black mud glistens, then rippling, as the water slips easily over the stones. I can feel it in my toes and my tingling breath. And when I open my eyes I know I have come back to myself.

'What a shame you didn't make anything at all today, dear,' says Miss Sheldon, looking sorrowfully at my ball of clay.

'It's all right, I don't mind.'

'Well, if you enjoyed yourself that's the main thing.'

'Yes, thank you, Miss Sheldon, I did.'

The windows are steaming up, the birds are beginning to trill and the evaporating mist is turning blue along with the sky. A pink moon has risen behind the trees. It looks like the heart of the sky.

Piggy says the last Mass is always longest. They want to fill you up with holiness to last the holidays. We have our heads bowed in lace mantillas, and stand solemnly in the pews, but everyone is excited inside.

The choir is weaving intricate patterns in the air, singing the Latin Mass they've been practising with Mother Perpetua for weeks. The candles are lighting up the gold on the altar, the air is filled with incense and singing, and soon I'll be free and see Very.

There is a new feeling too, a dull pain in my belly, legs as heavy as tree trunks, and I still feel ashamed. But talking to Very on the telephone has spread a light over everything, so even when Sister Gobnet raised her eyebrows and looked down that greasy nose with the wart on the side, when I asked her what to do about the stained sheet, I felt protected by the glow. She gave me a clenched-teeth look, and told me to take the sheet to Sister Ruth in the laundry room, so I had to carry it under my arm along the corridor, past everyone rushing down the stairs for Mass, and Sister Ruth wasn't in the laundry room, so I had to wait for Sister Helen to get her from the nuns' quarters.

Sister Ruth nodded without looking up when I explained to her. She was ashamed for me, and I had to run down those squeaking wooden stairs to be in time for Mass, and I'd reached the double queue breathless without my mantilla. A prefect had handed me a white lace one, and I'd walked down the side aisle and into the high voices and the flickering candlelight and now I'm sitting next to Sister Anne, and I'm not sure if I'm going to leak on to the wooden pew. It's everyone's worst fear to walk out of chapel with a stain on the back of their Function dress and not know. I look up at the statue of Mary – her smiling pink face gazes down modestly through big lids – and think, she's never had a period in her life.

The choir sings Kyrie eleison and Christi eleison and the aching threads of sound crack through the weight of the air and the whole sky comes rushing in. The voices leave their imprint on the air.

But I got through on the telephone. I got through, and I told Very the whole story. She said she knew something bad had happened because she'd opened the letter Mother Agatha had sent.

'You opened it, oh my God.'

'Well, yes, I wasn't going to forward it to Jakarta.'

'What did it say?'

'I've asked Mick to frame it so we can hang it in the loo.'

'Oh no, Very.' I suddenly have a horrible feeling that it could exude a Mother Agatha power or even give her the ability to see into the loo while we were sitting on it.

'Don't do that!'

'It's OK, Cath, I'm only joking. It just says what an appalling "and even dangerous" influence, blah blah blah.'

'But what did you write, Very? What was it?'

'I can't remember – it was that quote I read you in the park, remember? I copied that out.'

'The one saying that priests should be imprisoned?'

'Yes, you know, Nietzsche. I was going to send you the whole book, actually, but I thought it might get confiscated . . . and then what else, well, I think I might have told you about Big Terry's bail money. Oh I know what else – you know Tracy's in this band?'

'Yes.'

'Well . . . band, they keep smashing up all their instruments.'

'Yes, come on, tell me.'

'She's started writing songs, well, not exactly songs, shouts maybe. She's written one inspired by one of Brainy's football songs.'

'Oh?'

'Yes, I copied that out for you. I thought it would make you laugh.'

'Is it funny?'

'Well, it's a bit lewd.'

My heart sinks.

'What's it called?'

'The chorus goes something like "Fuck the Pope and the Virgin Mary",' and she sang it down the phone.

'Oh Very, say you didn't write that, please, say you didn't.'

'Sorry, Cath, when I come to think of it . . . I mean from their point of view . . .'

But she just started laughing.

'Oh Very.'

'Look, don't panic. You're out of there soon and you're coming to stay with me.'

'But they said I couldn't.'

'No, it's all right. Uncle Bill wrote saying he would collect you from the station, and he agrees I'm a bad influence.'

'Who's Uncle Bill?'

'Me, of course!'

I had to get her to explain it to me twice.

We sit down to listen to the sermon and Father Finnigan walks behind the lectern and raises up his hands to warn us against the indulgence of the holiday period.

'It's fashionable nowadays to think it's easy to get to heaven. Easy it is not!'

He fixes his eye on each girl in turn, and I know when he looks at me he's thinking, fourteen fish fingers.

'Life according to the flesh conflicts with life according to the spirit.'

He holds up his fist, his face reddens, and sweat stands out on his brow as he launches into a wobbling speech about the battle, the conflict, and the fight, against temptation, the world and the flesh. He points at the ceiling and the floor and spits into the air.

He calls on Jesus to descend into the human heart with the greatest of all weapons, love, so he may be our final victory, and whatever temptations affect us we can march along the road to heaven. Then he holds on to the lectern with both hands and everyone is relieved because he has spent his fury and looks tired.

The singing voices begin and call alongside each other on different notes. They dispel the battle and between them carry me into lovely and haunting places. The songs thread through one another like coloured ribbons colliding and combining to make ever more beautiful sounds.

I hear '*Deum de Deo*' and '*Lumen de lumina*' and a wall of high and low notes moves slowly along making a transforming shape in the air. The voices call higher and higher then hum low down undulating like a sea and quietening into one slow voice calling, minor, longing, then in a chorus, high up and fading into silence. Suddenly there is a great surge of '*Sanctus, sanctus, sanctus*', and the organ plunges and the voices rise up and I am breathless with the light pouring through the cracks, and my legs feel like tree trunks, and my head has opened like a flower and I don't even mind this big thing that happened to me in the night because after Mass I'm catching the train, and soon I will see Very.

'How many seconds now, Olive?'

'One thousand seven hundred and sixty-three,' says Olive slowly, looking at her watch.

We are sitting on the steps waiting for the taxi-van. I can smell the creosote on the art hut. We've said goodbye to Mother Agatha and Reverend Mother. You have to do a little curtsy. They'd all stood in a row. Sister Campion had patted my hand and kept it in hers, smiling at me with a kind of nodding pity.

Mother Agatha says a little bit of scripture to each girl in turn. She took my hand and while she held it she looked me right in the eye. I was so worried she'd read 'Very is collecting me from the station' written in my eyes that I kept blinking.

' "What does it profit a man to gain the whole world, if he suffer the loss of his own soul," ' she said in a stern voice.

Poor man, I thought. I couldn't see how it applied to me.

A horse neighs in the field behind the trees and Lucy who is up on the red-brick wall jumps off so her skirt flies up, lands with a smack, gets up, neighs too and starts riding round as if she is a horse. She stops, pulls out her sherbert fountain and sticks the liquorice in her mouth loaded with sherbert.

'I'm going to show the taxi man my bottom!' she says with the liquorice in her mouth, and brays like a donkey, 'HEE HAW, HEE HAW.'

'Lucy, for God's sake calm down or we'll get allocated an Upper Five.'

'Yeah, Lucy, grow up!'

But Lucy's been crazy for two days. When I walked down the corridor after talking to Very on the phone I'd heard the singing in the classroom and went to join in:

> One more day to go,
> One more day of sorrow,
> One more day in this old dump,
> And we'll be home tomorrow.

Lucy was up on the desk with her skirt over her head showing everyone her belly dance. She had a moustache from the Cherryade she was hiding behind her back. Sister Campion came in to tell us to quiet the noise, and when Lucy said, 'Sorry, Sister,' and jumped off the desk the Cherryade fizzed over the edge of the bottle all over the floor just as Sister closed the door.

Everyone said, 'Oh Lucy!'

We'd spent the day cleaning the classrooms, wiping the inkstains off the floor with that smelly floor cloth and brushing pencil shavings from the corners of our desks. Brain-box Olive hands me the Rubik's cube and I mix it up for her again and hand it back.

I have an ache in my belly, and I close my eyes. I feel

as if I'm being pulled downwards under river currents and the water has closed over the top and I am deep below the surface, where it is still. I open my eyes and everything is shimmering as though it is made of dots. We had to sweep the mud out of the cloakroom lockers too, and put the brown cloak and the hockey stick, the wellingtons, the outdoor shoes, into the gingham sheet, then there was a race down the polished corridor and out the arched door to the hockey hut to collect the hockey boots. It was only when they'd been cleaned and inspected that we could take the sheet to the gym and walk across the squeaky floor with springs in it to pack it all into a trunk.

I had to go to the art hut to find my clay woman. Her arms had fallen off in the kiln. She was standing behind a row of Third Form's thumb pots. Miss Sheldon said it happened to the Venus de Milo but it didn't cheer me up. Very said we could make some new ones out of Das but they'd be grey. I said grey arms are better than nothing. I wrapped her in a towel and took her up to the dorm.

The birds are singing in the lime trees. We climb into the taxi-van and there are tears and hoots and 'Write in the holidays', 'See you next term, worse luck', 'Write, please write', 'You know I will, moron'. There is a cheer when we drive through the school gates and Lucy lifts up her feet to show the passers-by her legs and the driver says, 'None of that, please, young ladies.'

When the train arrives we scramble on. I sit next to Olive and look out the window. It begins to move slowly then fast, I watch the town slipping away, then a wide plain stretches out with low hills in the distance, fences change their angles and cows flash by and rusted-roofed barns, then a ploughed field, and we pass under a bridge and the black shadow flits across my face.

I was sitting next to Sister Anne in chapel. The air was filled with incense and singing and I couldn't help looking at her out of the corner of my eye while she was praying. Her veil was flung back and I could see the curve of her long swan neck. She held her face with tender fingers, as though it was suffering and needed to be held that way. I could see her forehead wrinkled up, hidden behind her hands. Her eyes twitched. I wanted to shake her arm and say, 'Don't listen to that one, it's the wrong voice.'

That's when I looked up at the statue, and saw Mary's face change. I'd been shocked by the blood, by the big red stain, by Sister Gobnet's disgust and Sister Ruth's shame, but I didn't know what had come over me when I looked up and saw Mary's face turn black. I thought something had gone wrong with my eyes. The statue was turning into colours. I couldn't see her details, only her shape, and inside the shape were geometric patterns made of light and changing, like looking into a kaleidoscope. It all happened quickly, then she turned black. Her whole body was black, her breasts were naked and she looked straight at me. I closed my eyes. It's OK, it's the Black Madonna, I said to myself, and when I opened them she was back to normal.

But I can still feel her look. It had reached right in

me and I can still feel it all the way down to my feet. It was the same feeling I had that night when Juanita Fernandez rang the firebell as a prank and we'd all trooped out of the dormitory in our dressing gowns, down the squeaking wooden stairs, the nuns in black down to the ground, and the white faces of the girls scared out of sleep. The quiet shuffling, the whispered 'No talking!' and along the corridors into the chilly night to line up and be counted in the courtyard outside the chapel. And I'd looked at the glimmering stars in the clear night, and in one tiny moment of freedom the huge indigo night slipped through me. It was like that, as though the night sky was in me and she'd woken it up with her eyes.

A forest of naked trees flashes by and through it I see the clouds moving slowly and behind them the sun stays still and slides across the surface of the river at the same speed as the train.

Lucy leans over the seat in front and offers me her sucked liquorice. She doesn't like liquorice so when the sherbert's finished being sucked off she doesn't know what to do with it.

I shake my head.

'No thanks.'

She sticks a traffic light in her mouth and sucks it, still kneeling backwards in her chair. She takes out the traffic light and coughs loudly.

'Oh Lucy, germs, for God's sake!' says Hen.

'Gotta joke!' says Lucy. 'Listen, listen.' She puts the lolly back in her mouth and looks round at everyone.

'Two nuns driving in a car, right. A vampire lands on the windscreen. One says, "Show him your cross."' She takes out the lollipop. 'So the other one shouts, "Get off the windscreen, you wanker!"' And she bursts into loud guffaws. 'D'you get it – show him you're cross? D'you get it?'

'Oh shut up, Lucy!' says a chorus.

I see it first as the sky turns purple with the yellow lights and the brown buildings lit up with Christmas trees and flashing reindeer. Different-coloured threads of light are decorating the buildings and the lit-up windows. I can feel the change as though more thoughts are crowding the air, and the stations on the tube line flash past. I see a tube train outside its tube and I know I'm going to see Very soon and be walking with her down the pink pavement lit with yellow light and blue shadows.

You have to take time to leave, you leave second by second, Olive knows, but when you arrive you arrive all at once with a long screech and a clunk and the doors open and a woman is talking in echoes across the faraway arched ceiling announcing our arrival.

Very is here somewhere in this crowd. Very is here in her new boots and shorn-off peroxide-blonde hair. She said Eddie dyed it with a toothbrush. I look for her among the crowd of mothers in hairbands. We crowd and jostle on to the platform. The air smells of metal and smoke and oil. The uniformed girls disperse as some are picked off by waiting parents and the rest of us try to find our trunks and haul them on to trolleys. Some girls have got brothers to do it for them.

Olive and I put our trunks on the same trolley for company and because we are both shocked by the train that screeched to a halt and disgorged us into this huge ribbed hall that smokes and wheezes and echoes with incomprehensible voices.

'It's my dad,' says Olive quietly. She waits for him to run down the platform.

I feel a sudden pang that she is going. We shift her trunk on to another trolley and wave goodbye to each other. I watch her brown blazer until it has disappeared into the crowd.

Then I catch sight of the bright-orange hair. She's running through the people in that stripy jersey and the old turquoise skirt, but on her feet she's wearing a brand-new pair of black suede boxer's boots, with red laces. There is a barrier in the way and she can't get by it, so she climbs over with her big sketch book in one hand, and next thing you know I'm smelling the patchouli oil on her neck.

I had three things to tell her: I'd got my period, there's no hell, but it was in the street, after we'd blown two days' money on that one long taxi ride, and travelled through the strings of colours that lit up the dark towards Christmas and walked through the cold whistling night smelling London's burnt air, that I tried to tell Very the third thing and realised there are some things you can't say.

*   *   *

'Put it sideways. No, you get that end and put it sideways.'

'Ow!'

'OK, hang on a minute, push it round.'

'Fuck!'

'I said push.'

'I did push, it won't fit.'

'It will, I've done it before.'

The trunk thuds against the wall and we look at each other with round eyes hoping the noise won't bring the growling man from his lair in his brown dressing gown. When he snarls his lip curls back over his teeth like a dog.

After we've stowed the trunk under the hall table, and we've clambered up the narrow stairs, Very decides it's time to make something to eat. Very only cooks breakfast.

'You're going to get scurvy,' I say.

'No I'm not!' she says, and puts the jar of marmalade in front of my plate and taps its lid. She pushes a piece of toast through the bars of the rats' cage, and there's a scuffling and nibbling.

I'm sitting on the stairs, eating. I'm still in my brown uniform. The kitchen smells of bacon. I finish my plate and put it in the sink that looks on to the brown night and the thread of lit-up beads. She pats my back. She's eating off the sideboard and she's got a sausage in her mouth.

'It's orange. I was expecting blond.'

She holds a bit of the hair and looks at it sideways, and bites the sausage.

'Yeah, he didn't leave the peroxide on long enough, I think it makes me look green.'

'That's the scurvy,' I say.

She laughs.

We put the plates in the sink and make tea and clomp down the narrow stairs into the sitting room. It's all there. Just the same. The blue carpet with more fluff on it, the smell of oil paint and turps, and Very's easel set up with a new canvas on it, the tubes of oil paint scattered on a white sheet.

The turquoise terrapin is still in an aquarium on the mantelpiece, but she's given Old George back his nine eels so at least we can have a bath.

'I've got to get this off,' I say, and take off all my uniform even before I drink my tea.

Very throws a long shirt at me spattered with paint.

'Fresh from the launderette,' she says.

And I fall on to the cushions on the floor with a huge sigh. I can feel fronds unfurling round me as though I'm expanding out of a clenched-up ball.

'Oh Very!'

Suddenly with her there everything at the convent looks smaller, but I can still feel Mother Agatha's threads attached to me like a spider. They are thin but made of iron. I want to dance about to get free of them.

Very offers me a cigarette.

The telephone rings and Very answers.

'Hello, Eddie, yeah, about an hour ago.' She looks at me. 'Better by the minute.'

I can see piles of fluff and feathers under the sofa, and a collection of lost objects.

'No, we don't have a penny,' says Very. She puts her hand over the receiver and says, 'Eddie says Juliet's having a party and we're invited. Winnie'll be there.'

Maybe there's something useful in there by that cotton reel, and I look closer into the sofa's underneath darkness.

'Not even a bus fare,' she says to the telephone. 'I know it'll be a laugh, Eddie, it's just we don't . . .'

'Very, is that a pound note under there?'

'Hang on,' she says to Eddie.

She kneels to peer underneath and I pull out a piece of paper I can see sticking out of the spring.

'How did that get there?' she says, as I pull out a tenner.

'Who cares?' I say.

'Yeah, we will,' she says to Eddie. 'We will! Come round!'

She slams the phone down, puts *Never Mind the Bollocks* on the record player, and we pogo round the room with the needle jumping.

A NOTE ON THE AUTHOR

Helena McEwen is the author of *The Big House*.
She lives in London.

A NOTE ON THE TYPE

The text of this book is set in Linotype Janson. The original types were cut in about 1690 by Nicholas Kis, a Hungarian working in Amsterdam. The face was misnamed after Anton Janson, a Dutchman who worked at the Ehrhardt Foundry in Leipzig, where the original Kis types were kept in the early eighteenth century. Monotype Ehrhardt is based on Janson. The original matrices survived in Germany and were acquired in 1919 by the Stempel Foundry. Herman Zapf used these originals to redesign some of the weights and sizes for Stempel. This Linotype version was designed to follow the original types under the direction of C. H. Griffith.